Gowns & Gavels

Working for Love, Book 4

Amber W. Lynne

Carnelian & Quills Publishing

Edited by: Krissy Espindola (KrissyEspindola@gmail.com)
Cover Art by: Rebecca Ruger (BeckandDot@gmail.com)
Paper: ISBN 978-1-960479-31-0
eBook: ISBN 978-1-960479-30-3
Text Copyright © 2025 by Carnelian & Quills Publishing
All rights reserved.

This one's for Helen.
Who's seen me at my worst, laughed with me at my best, and
offered sage counsel in the moments between.

Thanks for riding the highs and lows with me. Bestie, I'm
ridiculously lucky to share this messy, wonderful life with you.

Chapter One

Taylor

The sequined hem sparked pinpoints of light that danced like fire.

Taylor sat in the front row of New York Fashion Week, her knees modestly angled, hands clenched so tightly they ached. Her gaze fixed on the model walking down the runway.

The gown's silver and rose-gold threads caught the light in a deliberate rhythm, making it feel like watching poetry walk in heels.

Bailey leaned in close, voice low and dry. "That one looks like she could conquer the world in stilettos and still send thank-you cards."

Candy grinned as she bit into a pistachio macaron. "She looks like she'd drive that stiletto straight through the heart of the first man dumb enough to cross her. I wish I had the guts to wear clothes like that."

On Taylor's other side, Molly, always composed, didn't smile but lifted her sparkling water in agreement. "Three votes yes."

Taylor tried to follow their lively conversation and stay present in the moment. "Candy, you could wear glitter every day if you wanted," she murmured, but her throat tightened, and her smile faded slightly at the edges.

When the music changed, another model glided by. She was wrapped in midnight blue tulle that whispered along the floor—the flared fabric draped at her hip in asymmetrical lines. Taylor's fingers twitched as if they held a pencil and were ready to trace the flowing lines of the dress.

A detail on her next look tightened the muscles in her neck. It had beaded cuffs shaped like satin vines, winding upward from the wrist. She'd drawn that cuff. In a sunlit room she used to rent...years ago, when she still believed in the beauty of fashion more than the politics behind it.

Her past was wearing stilettos and striding down the runway.

"Favorite so far?" Bailey nudged.

Taylor blinked. "I...don't know. They just all blur together."

A lie. She remembered each one—every line, every curve, every sketch scrawled into margins when she should have been working another shift. They were her lifeline, built in stolen hours, clung to in places that reeked of mold and old carpet. To pretend otherwise was to wear fragile armor. To admit she watched her dreams parade down the runway with someone else's name stitched to them...that was unbearable.

The show moved forward relentlessly. Chiffon trenches drifted past like storm clouds. Heavy gowns sparkled with beadwork so detailed she could almost feel the weight pulling at her shoulders. They were flawless. They were hers, and now, they belonged to him.

Taylor clapped when she had to, her palms hitting without feeling. She refused to look at the program, refused to let her eyes rest on the bold, confident font announcing the collection. His name would break her. Pretending not to see it was all she had left.

Then the last model appeared.

Everything stopped.

The blonde wore a pleated capelet shaped like butterfly wings. Wings Taylor had sketched while humming along to her mother's favorite opera in a swampy apartment, scissors dull against cheap fabric. The silhouette was unmistakable.

Taylor's breath stalled. Her hand pressed flat against her blouse as if pressure alone could keep her together, but inside, something tore. A rip that had started years ago, splitting open seam by seam under the floodlights.

Anger came first. Slow. Heavy. A betrayal that set her jaw hard.

Laurent Delacroix.

How dare he parade her gown—exactly as she'd conceived it—before New York Fashion Week? Without a single stitch of acknowledgment for her work?

She watched as the model pivoted at the end of the catwalk, the butterfly wings spreading, exaggerating the woman's movement. Taylor's hand fell to her lap, fingers curling into fists. He hadn't just stolen a sketch. He'd stolen her past. Her pride. Now, he was coasting off the very soul of her work while people sipped champagne and wrote little hearts beside his name in their stylists' notebooks.

And yet, it wasn't truly a surprise. That's what made it harder to accept. Somewhere inside, buried beneath layers of grief and self-doubt, she had expected this. Laurent Delacroix doesn't mentor prodigies—he consumes them. He draws them in, warms himself at the fire of their talent, and then snuffs out their spark before they can ignite.

She'd once admired him. At one point, she believed his smile showed approval, and that the way he lingered over her seam work and studied her pleats meant he understood her vision.

He'd seen something, all right. He'd recognized her worth, and then he waited for her to overlook it so he could take it for himself.

Her throat dried up. Her vision narrowed. Applause erupted around her. Flashes flickered at the edges of her sight. Reviewers whispered. Stylists scribbled. Taylor sat frozen.

When the music fell away and silence pressed in, she couldn't stay seated. Her body rose before her mind caught up, shame and disbelief blurring together.

She slipped into the aisle, careful not to stumble, arms trembling anyway. Sequined gowns brushed against her legs as she moved past champagne flutes and crossed ankles. She kept her eyes down. Couldn't speak. Couldn't let out the hot pressure burning its way to her throat.

She needed a way out.

A slit in the velvet curtain revealed stage lights. She pushed through.

Backstage hit like a slap. Glaring fluorescent lights, racks of silver metal, hairspray hanging in the air, stylists barking over dryers—a machine in full motion. Taylor moved through it invisibly, threading past tulle and sequins.

She ducked behind a wall of plastic-wrapped cocktail gowns. Her shoulder clipped a rack, sending a lookbook clattering to the ground. She winced but didn't stop.

She needed a corner—a second to breathe.

Pressed flat against the drywall, between garment bags and a makeup mirror, she forced her back rigid, struggling to hold herself together.

Hot tears startled her. She wasn't crying—she refused to cry—but the prickling proof was there, blurring the mascara she'd so carefully applied only hours earlier. She swiped at her face with the heel of her palm, angry at how fast it had all fallen apart.

"Oh my God," she whispered. "It's happening."

Not the theft—she'd already known about that—but the remembering.

The hem of that final gown dragged something from the past. Her history unraveled like a torn seam. Her old studio, her notebooks, the summer she had poured everything into an assignment she thought would launch her career. She ran away from it all, stayed silent for years, and convinced herself that silence was more thoughtful than fighting Laurent Delacroix.

But sitting in that chair, watching her own work parade down the runway under someone else's spotlight? It shattered the final remnants of her already fragile ego.

"Taylor?"

Candy's voice cut through.

Taylor's head snapped up as her friend rounded the corner, wide-eyed, slowing when she saw the hiding spot.

"I—" Taylor's voice cracked. "I had to get out."

"Okay." Candy's brows knit. "What happened?"

Taylor's laugh was thin, dying almost immediately. "I didn't think it would hit like this. I thought I'd see him, see the similarities, feel bruised. Maybe jealous. Not—"

"An ex?"

"No. My old mentor." She struggled to find the words to tell Candy how much he had meant to her. He was more than just a teacher, almost like a father, and definitely caused more damage than an ex. "He was the reason my life fell apart. It just—"

"Shattered?"

She nodded, eyes glossy again.

"It wasn't just a gown," she whispered. "It was my past. The dreams I boxed up. The sketches I told myself weren't worth keeping, and I realized...they didn't stay buried. He pulled them into the spotlight and took the applause, and I let him."

Candy stepped in beside her, quiet, holding out a tissue.

Taylor took it.

"I thought it would be okay. I've moved on!" she said, looking around. "But my past was here waiting for me."

Chapter Two

Taylor

She rubbed her forehead, palm damp with the adrenaline still pulsing through her. The beading. The sculpted hem. She'd memorialized every detail in a sketchbook that hadn't opened in years because she'd buried it in a drawer back in Serenity.

The pastel organza on the rack beside her swayed, and she pressed her shoulder into it, grounding herself.

Candy sat close, fingers worrying the corner of a tissue. Her eyes flicked toward Taylor, unsure what to say, but unwilling to leave. "I texted Bailey. She's worried."

The buzz of the backstage chaos continued, a hurricane of models, stylists, and interns spinning around them.

Then footsteps.

"Taylor?" Bailey's voice rang out, sharp and searching.

Moments later, Bailey and Molly appeared from around the corner, breathless and alert, crowding into the narrow aisle between a garment steamer and a stack of plastic-wrapped gowns.

Molly's brows jumped. "What are you doing back here? We lost you after the finale."

Bailey's gaze dropped to where Taylor was half crouched beside the garment rack, pale and trembling. "Are you okay?"

Candy gave them both a look and answered. "She's not hurt. Just...a little gut punched."

Bailey sank down beside them. "Taylor, what happened?"

Taylor swallowed, her voice low, like it was still coming from very far away. "It wasn't just a dress."

"What wasn't?" Molly asked, studying her face.

Taylor stared at the floor. "The collection. The beading. The butterfly collar. All of it. Every last stitch was mine."

Bailey's posture went stiff. "Yours?"

Taylor nodded. "Designs I never published. Sketches I only ever shared with one person."

"Who?" Molly's voice was even, but the steel beneath it showed.

Taylor's lips trembled. "Laurent Delacroix. He stole my designs."

The air shifted.

Bailey's tone sharpened. "You're telling me the show we just watched was built off your work?"

Taylor let out a hollow laugh. "Built off them? Try mirrored. Right down to the cuff work."

Candy's cheeks flushed. Her earrings swung as she leaned in. "Do you want a cookie? You look like you need protein, or a margarita."

Taylor didn't answer. Her mouth was dry.

Molly glanced back toward the staging entrance. "Photographers were filing in backstage. I think Delacroix knew how to stage that last dress for maximum drama."

Taylor's voice faltered. "My gown..." Sugar and bile spiraled in her stomach. The dressing room around her, glowing with the efforts of a dozen makeup mirrors and ring lights, suddenly blurred. She gripped the edge of a rolling rack to steady herself.

Bailey's arm shot out to keep her steady. "Talk. Now."

Taylor nodded, breath catching. "I'd know that gown blindfolded. Senior year in LA. My capstone collection. I saw at least three other designs in the lookbook. That dress came from a sketch I only ever showed him. He said it was foolish. It was too feminine, too soft for the market." Her gaze went distant, reliving every critique. "I trusted him. He told me they were exercises. That critiques were private, but he still used them."

"You didn't tell us this might happen," Bailey said, fury simmering under her voice.

"I thought maybe it was in my head," Taylor said. "Or that no one would believe me. I was twenty-three, humiliated, broke, and too proud to tell anyone. I packed up and left LA because every time I walked into a classroom, I felt like I didn't belong there anymore."

Her hands twisted in her lap, thumbs tracing the thin scar on her knuckle from a rotary blade, earned in the blur of that last semester.

"I remember the day perfectly," she added. "The classroom smelled like starch and old drafting paper. We were all lined up in front of the critique platform. Laurent Delacroix walked through like royalty, adjusting pleats and collars, passing judgment. My portfolio was last."

Her gaze dropped with the weight of the memory.

"I'd stayed until two in the morning. Sketches pinned straight. Drapes labeled. I'd even stitched a miniature of my capstone dress. It had ivory lace over satin crepe, with a ribboned waist inspired by ballet armor. The fabric was soft, but strong. I wanted women to feel both."

She huffed a bitter sound. "He didn't even touch it. Just stared for a second, hands folded behind his back like I'd offered him a grocery list instead of a garment."

Bailey and Candy stayed silent, eyes fixed on her.

"He said, 'It's feminine, but irrelevant.' Then told me I was dressing paper dolls. Said a woman wanted to be wanted, not to twirl in opera capes. That my work was sentiment, not design."

Her throat tightened. "He told me everything I had, that all I was, was *sweet*. Not sharp. Not structured. Not planned."

Her voice cracked.

"And I believed him. I really did. I packed up my needles, my sketchbooks...everything, and I left the city thinking I'd been foolish to try."

Taylor blinked hard, forcing the memory back into place.

I never told anyone because I thought I'd overreacted, because if someone you admire says you're forgettable, that softness is weakness instead of a choice..." Her eyes lifted, glossed but steady. "You start to believe it."

Candy stepped nearer and placed her hand on Taylor's shoulder. "You buried it because it hurt too much to say it out loud."

Taylor nodded. Her voice was nearly a whisper. "I buried LA, and everything I made there."

For a moment, only the hiss of steamers and the click of cameras filled the alcove.

Molly angled her hips, blocking Taylor from the flow of people. "You're certain?"

"I can remember that hem clearly," Taylor said, closing her eyes briefly. "It's not just one piece. It's all of them. He didn't steal an idea, Molly. He stole my whole line."

Bailey shook her head, clearly furious. "We're not letting him get away with it."

Molly's voice was calm but sharp. "Not without a plan. Delacroix will be swarmed by the press the moment he steps off that runway. If we're going to make this story public, we need to stay smart."

"I'm not ready," Taylor said, breath shallow. "I don't have proof. I don't even know where to start—"

"You already started," Bailey cut in. "By telling us. You thought you were alone. You're not."

Taylor let out a broken laugh. "I didn't come here looking for a fight. I thought it would be nostalgic. Maybe inspiring, but not to be pulled into the past like a hostage."

"Well," Candy said, her own eyes wet, "then you're about to make one hell of a comeback from a very inconvenient flash-back."

Taylor's mouth trembled, but her spine straightened.

Only thirty minutes earlier, she'd been watching a runway with longing and grief. Now, the sharp edges of betrayal had carved that longing into something sharp. Focused.

If this was where the unraveling began—in a narrow make-up alcove surrounded by organza and truth—then so be it.

Bailey rose from her crouch, eyes already calculating. "Drinks first. Then a battle plan."

Chapter Three

Taylor

The lounge above the runway was swathed in velvet and shadow, a pocket of stillness suspended over the chaos of Fashion Week. Taylor perched on the edge of an ottoman, the light glinting off the rim of her untouched cocktail.

The air hummed with jazz and the scent of citrus and bourbon, but beneath the luxe velvet and low lighting, she still felt the spotlight. Not the kind with bulbs, gels, and applause, but the type that seared into your skin. The kind that came when people stared, let their silence drag out, and watched you while they waited for your voice to stop shaking.

She hated it.

"That was never public, right?" Bailey leaned forward. "Your senior collection? Any of those sketches online?"

Taylor shook her head. "No. We weren't allowed. The mentorship focused on creating physical portfolios. Delacroix was old school with charcoal sketches and hand-colored proofs. He hated screens. Said they weakened intuition."

Molly's eyes narrowed. "Convenient. You have no time-stamp. No uploads. He can claim anything."

Candy pushed a heavy glass of ginger soda toward Taylor. "Drink. You're pale."

The cool glass steadied her a little. She nodded a quiet thank-you and took a sip.

"For a long time, I thought maybe I was imagining it," Taylor said. "A trim here, a silhouette there. I told myself it was a coincidence, or worse, that I couldn't tell my voice from his anymore." She swallowed hard. "But that gown out there? That was mine. Start to finish. No edits. No tweaks. Just stolen, thread by thread."

Bailey didn't blink. "Then we prove it."

Taylor gave a short, dry laugh. "I handed him everything. Sketches. Fabric swatches. Process boards." Her voice grew hoarse. "I was young and so hungry. So grateful to be learning from Laurent Delacroix. He said I was his brightest. His 'pet project.' He used to brag to the other faculty that I had the instincts of a couturier already."

Her breath shuddered out. "We spent hours in studio critiques. He'd lean over my shoulder, adjust my lines, tell me, 'You could be someone, if you listen.' And I listened. I believed every word."

Candy and Bailey exchanged a glance. Molly didn't look away.

"I didn't see it until it was too late." Taylor's hands curled reflexively over nonexistent fabric, as if she needed something to hold onto. "In my final year, he asked me to show him my capstone sketches early. He only wanted the roughs to help refine them before the program submission deadline." She shook her head, anger and shame clashing in her voice. "A week later, at my critique, he trash-canned the whole thing in front of the class. Called it...utterly forgettable. Said I was too sentimental. That I dressed dreams instead of women."

"Coward," Candy muttered under her breath.

Taylor's eyes burned. "When I tried to salvage the project and resubmit something new, he blocked me. Said he wouldn't approve my credits. Said that if I couldn't handle feedback, then maybe I wasn't meant for fashion after all."

Bailey's jaw flexed.

"And then," Taylor said, her voice lower now, "six months after I left LA and moved to Serenity, his new collection debuted in Milan. Front cover of Vogue Italia. My silhouettes. My color stories."

"That asshole!" gasped Candy.

"There was one thing he never used," Taylor said. Her voice softened. "My signature."

Bailey leaned in. "Your label?"

"Sort of. I stitched a note into the linings. Small. Hidden. Just for the woman wearing it. My favorite was, 'For you. Not for the world.' It was for my Mom. She always said, 'You're not dressing the world. You're dressing the woman who survives it.' I embroidered it by hand in rose-gold thread."

Candy let out a soft breath. "Like a fashion love letter."

Taylor's mouth curved faintly. "Exactly. A wish whispered over cloth and string. I designed for the woman, not the runway."

Molly folded her arms. "And he left those out."

Taylor nodded. "I've never seen proof that he's used it. When he reviewed my work, he hated that the most. He never understood the soul of it. He took the sketches, the silhouettes, the technique, but not the voice. Not the intention. Art is communal. I can't lay claim to a hemline."

Her fingers curled as though she still felt the needle in her hand.

"I might've buried my name," she said, "but I never buried what I believed in. He took the art, not the heart."

She wasn't crying now, but the quiet that followed felt heavier than tears.

"It wasn't just that he stole the work," she said, like the words had barbs. "It was how easy it was for him to make me believe I didn't deserve it." Her fingers twisted into the hem of her sleeve, as if she was holding onto something solid. "I was never what the others were—draped in black, quoting design theory like scripture. I walked in with thread in my hair and calluses on my fingers."

Her laugh was sharp and humorless. "He made it seem like letting me in was charity. Like if I stayed quiet, I could ride on borrowed brilliance."

"How did you even get his attention?" Molly asked, calm but curious.

Taylor straightened. "I didn't have enough to attend the fancy programs, but I worked. I sewed for boutiques, fixed hems for professors, and filled every spare hour with a job. My mother was a cleaning woman. A single mom. We didn't do 'extra,' we did 'enough.'"

Candy's breath caught.

"She'd bring home the fancy clothes her clients didn't want anymore. It was always hand-me-downs or pieces with holes or stains. I'd resize them. Flip old velvet curtains into coats. Add a ribbon or feathery fringe if the seams were too thin."

She smiled at the memory, small and soft. "My Mom and I made my prom dress on a folding table with a borrowed machine. It had one working pedal and smelled like oil, but I felt like a queen in that dress."

Bailey pressed her lips together.

"So, when Delacroix noticed me? I thought it meant something. I thought someone finally saw what I saw, but now..." Her head shook slowly. "Now I realize it was about what he could take away."

Her gaze lifted, locking fully with Bailey's, then Molly's. "But the grit? The way I see fabric and shape? That came from watching my mother turn a donated wedding dress into a church suit. That's how I learned resurrection."

Her chin lifted. "Nothing was handed to me. So, he doesn't get to keep what I built."

"And now he's parading your 'practice' down a million-dollar runway like a group project where he did all the work?" Candy raised her martini. "Cheers to that."

Molly's voice was quiet but sharp. "Motive. Means. All we need is opportunity."

Bailey reached into her bag and pulled out a sleek leather planner. "Already ahead of you. We've already started," Bailey added. "This is just the strategy session."

Outside, Manhattan glowed. Inside, Taylor studied her reflection in the untouched drink and didn't look away. "What now? We storm downstairs and shout plagiarism from behind the flower wall?"

Bailey snorted.

"I can't sue him. No proof. No files, no witness, nothing but—" She cut off before heartbreak finished the sentence.

Bailey set her glass down. "That's not your problem. We'll make it Clinton's."

Molly, confused, asked, "Who's Clinton?"

"My faithful family corporate attorney," Bailey said. "Ruthless, charming, and deadlier than he looks in a three-piece suit. He's never let me down." Her voice grew serious. "I owe him my life. I wouldn't have made it this far without him."

"I've seen him work," Candy added. "Terrifying. Surgical, but effective."

"He's meeting us tomorrow," Bailey said, jotting notes. "If anyone's equipped to take on Delacroix's ego, it's Clinton Conners."

Taylor hesitated. "I don't want this to become public. I don't even know if I want to actually *do* anything. I didn't come back to change the past—"

Molly's voice was quiet and steady as it slipped in. "You didn't come for this. You came because it was your birthday. After all, you wanted to be with people who love you. You thought it was safe, but once you saw what he did, you couldn't unsee it."

That landed. Taylor blinked, eyes glossy.

"So, while you didn't come looking for a fight, maybe you're done pretending it never happened."

The truth pushed its way through her chest. She was supposed to be over it, but the moment that gown took the runway, every buried part of the girl she used to be clawed back into the light.

Molly's head tilted slightly. "You gave him something real, and now you get to decide what you do with that."

Taylor let the words settle.

Outside the window, Manhattan blinked in soft electric patterns. Somewhere out there was the runway she'd never walked. The collection she never finished.

Taylor turned her gaze back toward her friends, her voice still quiet but a little stronger this time. "Okay. One step. No press. No noise. Just...what's mine."

Bailey nodded. "We'll see Clinton tomorrow. Bring whatever you've got: sketches, portfolios, scraps. We'll strike quickly."

Taylor raised an eyebrow. "We?"

"Oh, honey," Candy said through a wide grin, "It won't be that easy to get rid of us."

Molly lifted her glass. "To take back what's yours."

Candy followed. "And doing it in fabulous shoes."

Taylor let her fingertips tap the rim of her own glass, then lifted it too. "Alright," she said, finally. "Let's sew some chaos."

Chapter Four

Clinton

Clinton Conners had been summoned to a wide range of situations in the service of the Reynolds family—some absurd, some borderline illegal, and most requiring more patience than precedent. He'd renegotiated distillery contracts mid-barbecue, smoothed over a scandal involving a misquoted bourbon label, and once extracted a client from a PR nightmare by pretending to be an estranged father.

But this? This was new.

Today, as he stood in the doorway of Bailey Reynolds' Chelsea loft—not a courthouse, not a boardroom, but a sun-drenched space strung with twinkle lights and curtain tie-backs fastened with tulips. He considered, not for the first time, that being the Reynolds family's de facto fixer required far more finesse than his Columbia Law education had prepared him for.

There were the odd-hour phone calls, such as the one he'd received yesterday: *Don't yell, but I might have promised a fash-*

ion designer you'd help with an intellectual property lawsuit.

Bailey seemed to find real pleasure in surprising him. Still, he liked her—her chaos and charm, her unwavering decisiveness paired with a complete disregard for formality. The fact that she preferred handwritten lists to spreadsheets was also notable. More than anything, he genuinely liked his job.

So, here he was. He adjusted the cuffs of his tailored sleeve and braced himself to meet whoever, or whatever, Bailey had decided she needed him to fix today.

The door swung open without warning.

Clinton blinked, surprised not by the timing but by the woman standing in front of him.

She radiated elegance. Her bare feet peeked out from beneath silk pants the color of stormy quartz, with the hem just brushing the brownstone's entryway floor behind her. A white cotton blouse, half-tucked and knotted at the waist, hung off one shoulder as if she'd been interrupted mid-outfit, yet it still looked like a fashion magazine cover. Dapping silver hoops caught the waning sun from the stoop, and her hair — braided then twisted into a halo knot — looked like something Botticelli might have tried to recreate if he'd had access to bobby pins and dry shampoo. Her lips remained bare. Her eyes were sharp.

Who's this?

She wasn't what he had been expecting. Not that Bailey had given him much warning about what to expect. She didn't usually. This woman was clearly not an assistant or one of Rosie's babysitters.

"Hello, I'm looking for Bailey," he said.

"Oh. I thought you were the lunch delivery." She peeked

past him and then turned over her shoulder to yell. "Bailey! I think Clint's here!"

Clinton blinked. *Clint?*

She turned back with a smile that froze him in place, then warmed his blood too quickly.

"Clinton Conners," he corrected, steadying his briefcase as he offered a hand. "Pleasure."

She didn't take his hand right away. Her eyes, steely blue, flicked to the briefcase. "I hope you have actual papers in there. It's my birthday, but I don't think Bailey would hire a stripper."

His mouth twitched, surprised by the flash of dry humor. "Let's start with introductions," he said calmly. "We can cover my briefs later."

That earned him a slight smile. "Taylor Rousseau." She stepped aside.

"Clint!" Bailey appeared from the kitchen, a coffee mug in one hand and a pen stuck in her bun like an afterthought. "You found us."

"Clinton," he muttered with long-suffering affection. It was a game they'd been playing for years. "I helped you close the papers to buy this place, of course, I found you."

"We made cinnamon knots!" Candy waved enthusiastically from a floral armchair, cheeks flushed from mimosas, and fingers dusted with powdered sugar. "Emotional support food. Help yourself!"

Clinton glanced down at the sprawling pile of sketchbooks, fabric tools, and coffee mugs. "This looks less like brunch and more like a war room."

"I call it couture triage," Taylor said, arms folded.

Her voice was soft, but edged with sarcasm, and Clinton filed that tone away instantly. He wouldn't mistake quiet for fragile.

Bailey gestured toward the couch. "Grab yourself a coffee and a snack." She waved at Molly and Candy. "We'll take a walk around the block and let Taylor tell you her story."

Clinton nodded. "Yes, that's a great place to start."

Taylor hesitated. The faintest tremor in her jaw betrayed the weight of the decision, as if she were still deciding whether saying it aloud again would make it hurt more, or make it real. After a long moment, she gave a single nod.

Clinton listened.

He didn't interrupt. Just let the words spool out, steady and sharp in her voice, even when they trembled at the edges. Her posture stayed composed—shoulders slightly rounded, fingers steepled over the open sketchbook on the coffee table between them—but there was a tension in the way she flexed her hand between gestures, as if the telling itself jabbed at old bruises long since disguised beneath calm.

Her voice carried weight as if each sentence had to decide whether to come out clean or cut on its way through.

She slid page after page across the table. Originals with smudged, annotated corners inked with stray lines of poetry. When she let out a shallow breath after showing him, the sound felt like a confession. Her eyes met his, waiting for judgment.

From a legal perspective, he knew the case would be complicated. Designs were often discarded, remade, blurred by in-fluence and trend. The courts weren't kind to creators with no paper trail, and yet...

Clinton tipped his head slightly and studied the sketchpad again. One sketch held him. It was a butterfly-wing capelet. The waist curved with precision. It was organic, technical, alive. He wasn't a fashion expert, but he knew mastery when he saw it.

It wasn't only the sketch that held him still, but the silence that followed. The small exhale she made as if she'd confessed something intimate, not just professional. Her eyes searched his, as if expecting a verdict.

Clinton adjusted his cuffs slowly. "You know this could be a long battle," he said. His tone was even, but his eyes didn't waver from hers. "Laurent Delacroix has resources and likely a legal team with more paper than the Vatican archives. He'll try to bury you before admitting theft."

Taylor arched an eyebrow and took a slow sip from the untouched tea Candy had thrust into her hands earlier. "You're trying to warn me off already?"

"I'm trying to make sure you know the weight of what you're lifting," he said. "People think court cases are about truth. They're not. They're about documentation. Timelines. Negotiated leverage."

She gave a soft snort. "And here I thought you might offer something more encouraging."

Clinton leaned back a fraction. "I could lie, if charming optimism is your language."

"Oh, no," she replied, mouth twitching into a half-smile. "I've had my fill of charming liars. I'll take strategic pessimism."

He tapped the sketchbook gently. "This one," he said, gesturing toward the butterfly-pleated piece. "Tell me about it."

Her fingers slowly followed his, resting just shy of the page's edge. "That was stitched on a carpet-covered ironing board in a guesthouse I sublet for eight weeks. Her fingers hovered near the page. "No heat, one window. My mom mailed me thrifted brocade, and I bartered for the rest. I was listening to an aria about broken wings. I wanted that feeling stitched into it."

His hand stilled.

Something quiet passed between them. A beat of recognition. He'd heard similar words in a different life. From someone who once believed her way through pain until the belief couldn't outrun the weight of perception anymore. Origin, not revision. Story, not trend.

"That's what he can't steal," Clinton said finally. "He copied the lines. He can't copy the soul."

Taylor blinked. She stared at him, as if she hadn't expected him to say it so plainly.

"And what's my legal argument?" she asked.

Clinton looked her in the eye, something unwinding in his chest before he answered.

"You're the source."

Taylor tilted her head. "And you believe me?"

He didn't look away. "I wouldn't be here if I didn't."

Something shifted. She leaned in just slightly, eyes brightening. "You always this convincing, Counselor?"

"Only when someone hands me prima facie evidence wrapped in lace and poetry," he replied, deadpan.

A soft laugh broke free from her lips. "You might be dangerous," she murmured.

Clinton arched a brow. "You walked me into a tea-stained war room in ankle-fraying pants and a halo bun and asked me to battle a narcissist with gallery press on speed dial. You might be the dangerous one."

Her grin spread, slow and surprised.

"I don't need him ruined," she said. "Just...something . Proof it wasn't all in my head."

Clinton angled forward slightly, notebooks between them, cups cooling.

Clinton leaned in, voice even. "I don't take every case personally, but this isn't about sales or applause. It's about erasure, and I don't tolerate watching women erased."

Taylor's eyes swept over him. If he was still trying to win her trust, he'd just closed the deal.

She reached for her tea and took a long sip. Then she looked at him over the rim. "You're pretty good at speeches, Counselor."

"I've been told," he said, settling back again, but his gaze lingered a moment too long.

"Do you always flirt across case files?" she teased.

"Do you always answer with questions?"

"Well," she said, drawing the syllable out as she closed the sketchbook slowly, "That depends. Are we still in a legal meeting? Or does this count as off the clock?"

Clinton's eyes flicked to the empty mug. Her hand still grazed the sketchpad, and she had the barest curve of amusement on her mouth.

They were both smiling now.

Clinton pulled a business card from the inner pocket of his charcoal blazer, not because she needed it, but because it gave his hands something to do.

He slid it across the coffee table, clean lines facing up.

"Call me when you find that sketchbook with his handwriting in it," he said. "And anything else you thought didn't matter until now."

Taylor took the card, turned it over once, and tucked it into the folds of her leather portfolio.

"I will."

The doorknob on the front door rattled before Bailey's voice called out, and the door swung open. "Got what you needed?" she asked, grinning as she ducked back into the loft.

Molly followed close behind, polished and unreadable as always, but her arched brow said plenty. "Well? Did you hire him? Or do we need to review his credentials over quiche?"

Candy trailed them both, walking to the kitchen to pour a fresh mimosa. "We gave you a whole fifteen minutes of lawyer-client privacy. That's generous for us."

Taylor rolled her eyes, but her smile tugged at the corner of her lips. "You said you were going for a walk."

"We walked to the end of the block and decided we were bored," Candy sniffed, plopping back into the floral armchair. "Besides, the vibe in here was too good to miss."

Bailey leaned in over Clinton's shoulder, eyes flicking to the sketch spread between them like a reporter sniffing out a lead.

"So?" she asked. "What can we do?"

Clinton, still seated, pen poised, tablet open, looked up and took them in one by one with a composure that could only be cultivated through years of dealing with emotionally invested clients and the occasional bespoke fire drill.

"Technically," he said, "Ms. Rousseau is my client, but I'll allow non-binding input from the committee."

Taylor scrubbed her face, half amused, half mortified. "Please, let him work."

"Well, you didn't actually think we'd leave you alone with someone that attractive with only a legal pad between the two of you," Candy said, mock offended.

Clinton cleared his throat lightly, expression neutral, though a corner of his mouth twitched. "There's currently no lawsuit, but there might be with some groundwork."

"Is there documentation that he had access to your designs?" he asked, much calmer than the peanut gallery surrounding him.

Taylor crossed her arms. "Aside from transcripts showing he was my teacher? No. Everything else was context. I handed him everything. He saw the notebooks. Even made notes in the margins sometimes."

"You still have those notes?" he asked.

"I'm not sure," she admitted. "A lot's been boxed and stored since I left LA, but my mom saves everything. She was afraid I'd throw it all out. There's a chance she still has something."

Molly folded her arms, satisfied. "We can find those. Next?"

Clinton held up a hand, patient as a priest at confession. "Let's walk through what we're building, what you want. What you're willing to risk."

Candy leaned forward, eyes bright. "We want her name in lights and his ego on a platter."

Bailey grinned at Taylor. "But we'll settle for justice, and some new designs...the holidays are coming. Maybe something in velvet."

Clinton offered the faintest smile, but his focus remained on Taylor. "No copyright filings? No trademarks?"

"No. That was the whole point of that final semester. We were going to build a portfolio, an identity, and anchor a brand. I never got the chance."

He nodded once. Efficient. He'd seen people lose fortunes over stolen intellectual property, but their losses lived in spreadsheets, not in sketchbooks.

"You've already lost your voice once," he said carefully, folding his hands over the portfolio. "We're going to do everything we can to make sure he can't keep it."

"He's not going to back down," Clinton continued. "Delacroix's brand thrives on exclusivity and perception. You're a story he buried five years ago. Now, you're a threat. If you go public, he'll either try to discredit you or settle quietly to avoid the mess."

"Settle?" Taylor bristled. "You think I want hush money?"

"I think you deserve choices," he said, tone even but pointed.

Bailey cleared her throat. "What if we play this on two fronts?"

Clinton turned toward her. This wasn't new; Bailey had already floated the idea, but saying it here, in front of Taylor, was strategic. Bailey was always two steps ahead.

"Operation Mystique," Bailey said. "We unveil Taylor's new designs. Quietly. Through clients and Influencers. No name. No face. Just clothes. Her brand."

Molly, now leaning against the wall, chimed in. "I like it. We provoke buzz with better work. Let the market decide whose vision is evolving."

Clinton looked to Taylor. "It's not a legal counterattack, but it might buy you time. Build credibility. If you decide to pursue this formally, you'll want irrefutable proof, and a brand identity the public already recognizes."

"Copiers only copy," Candy said. "Delacroix can't compete. The style was never his. He has nothing new to say."

Taylor exhaled and rubbed the back of her neck.

"I'm not trying to pressure you," Clinton added, "But I know this much: bullies prosper because of politeness. If you stay quiet, he wins."

Another long pause. Then, softly, Taylor said, "Alright."

"We'll have clients sign NDAs. I'll form an LLC and start filing ownership documents," Clinton said, already scribbling. "We'll keep your identity under wraps, but start to establish you as the originator. Until then, everything stays in this circle."

"Secrecy is our greatest weapon," Bailey said.

Taylor looked at him. "Thank you. I didn't think I'd feel excited after talking."

Clinton gave a nod. "I'm very good at reminding people what they actually own," he said, his gaze flicking to the sketches. "And what they should never have given away."

She smiled at that, small but real.

"Once you're operational, I need the originals of these sketches," he said, tapping the nearest one. "They'll strengthen the case file, and it's impressive work."

Taylor arched a brow. "Surprised I can draw?"

"I've been surprised by a lot of things today," he said honestly. "But mostly, I'm relieved you didn't let him take everything."

She gave a soft laugh, eyes drifting toward the portfolio. "Not for lack of trying."

Clinton hesitated at the threshold, not quite ready to leave. Most clients were puzzles, problems to untangle, or motives to map. Taylor felt different. A puzzle made of color and texture. Less work. More art.

"You're different from my usual clients," he said before he could stop himself.

Taylor looked up, amused. "Because of the tattoos?"

"No, because you're not fighting from the sidelines. You're already on the line."

Behind him, thunder rolled.

He gave a brief nod, slipping back into professional mode. "Keep everything you can find. Originals. Notes. Fabric swatches. I'll pick them up at the same time tomorrow."

Taylor's lashes dipped as she nodded. "Clint?"

He paused, almost replied, then said, "Yes?"

"I'm glad you said yes."

So was he—more than he should be.

Chapter Five

Taylor

If the number of times she'd signed her name that morning was any indication, what Taylor had just done was bigger than she let herself believe.

Mystique Designs, LLC.

Taylor stared at the freshly filed paperwork and admired her name printed in a clean serif font across the top.

She'd signed everything in Bailey's kitchen on a marble-swirled island sticky with cinnamon glaze. Clinton hadn't rushed her. He didn't seem like a man who rushed anything. He'd pointed, explained, and waited with a composure that made her think maybe this was possible.

He'd closed the gold-ringed folder with that velvety precision of his and said, "You're official now."

The moment felt bigger than she had expected. Not because it came with champagne or confetti, but because it didn't. It was quiet. Uncomplicated. Something inside her shifted.

She knew about firsts. She was the first in her family to

pursue higher education, a first-time business owner of A Stitch in Time, and the first to leave Texas, although she ultimately returned, not to her hometown, but to her roots. Maybe she was good at starting, but not so good at finishing. This was something she wanted to see through.

She'd thought her small-town boutique would be it...her way of making the world more beautiful and staying connected to the threads and textures that fed her soul. One trip out of town, and her shop was now a quaint project, and she was a NY designer. She didn't know what she was doing. Her life had exploded overnight, and here she was trying to figure out what the next right thing was.

Across the room, Bailey tapped furiously on her phone while Candy and Molly perched on either side of the couch, each with a different bubbly drink in hand and matching grins that held Cheshire cat energy. They were enjoying every bit of what they were witnessing.

"Wait. Listen," Bailey called, holding up a hand as another response pinged in.

Taylor leaned forward. "Who now?"

Bailey grinned like the devil had just promised a brand deal. "Jalisa Grant. She just said, and I quote, 'Count me in. If I'm not the first to see this new designer, you can cancel my RSVP to the Purpose Gala.'"

Taylor blinked. "Isn't that the $25,000-a-table youth mentorship event?"

"Exactly," Bailey grinned. "She's threatening to skip philanthropy for fashion. We've created a monster."

Candy whooped. "She's unhinged! I fully respect it."

"Oh, and Gita Sheng responded," Bailey said, scrolling. "Seventeen flame emojis. One dancing cat."

"High praise," Molly murmured, swirling her sparkling water. "The cat is her 'I'm in' emoji."

"Well, she's been widowed three times. I think her cats are all she has left. I'll get her to commit to a fitting date."

Taylor blinked. "I don't understand how the algorithm works anymore."

"You don't have to," Bailey said, handing her a glass of champagne. "They want in. They love the aesthetic, but they have no idea who you are. You're just Mystique. You, my love, are officially the secret red-hot commodity on their must-wear list."

Taylor took a careful sip of her champagne, her fingers wrapped tightly around the delicate stem. "So...this is happening."

"Women with six-figure Influencer followings are lining up to wear gowns you sketched under a flickering desk lamp above a consignment store in one of the smallest towns in Texas. I'd say this is very much happening."

"It doesn't feel real."

"Give it time," Molly said. "It's about to."

Taylor smiled, soft but guarded. "I still don't know if I can do this."

"Can? You already are," Bailey said. "You've jumped."

She nodded, swallowed, leaned back against the couch, and let the voices wash over her.

Around her, Bailey's loft was a mess of fabrics and sketchpads and laughter-softened voices. She'd let Taylor take over as her new life as Mystique launched. Clinton had left hours ago with a calm, "I'll see you later this week, but you know how to reach me if you need me. I'll send the NDA packets tonight." But not before letting his hand brush hers, just long enough to say more than he had aloud.

Taylor had watched him leave out the door with his overcoat collar flipped up against the fall wind, and something not entirely unfamiliar had twisted behind her ribs. Hope. It had just been a really long time since she had felt it.

Now, she was going to hold on to it tightly. The girls were going home early tomorrow morning—back to Serenity, to Patty Cakes, and kindhearted small-town chaos—but tonight they were here, and she didn't want to waste a second of it.

Bailey crossed her legs and waggled her phone triumphantly. "Five confirmed clients. NDA-signed. Fittings scheduled. We're...what's the appropriate business term? Killin' It?"

Molly tilted her head. "You're positioning yourself as a ghost brand. Limited touchpoints. No ID, just design and silhouette. It's perfect. Laurent Delacroix won't even know he's chasing you until it's too late."

Taylor swirled her champagne idly. "Do you think people will care, once they find out it was me?"

"Eventually." Molly's tone was deceptively mild.

Taylor sighed. "Clinton said something earlier. Right before he left, he said, 'You're not a fake name. You're an entire brand.' What does he mean by that?"

Bailey let out a low whistle. "That man has lines."

"Oh! He's more than handsome. He's deep, too." Candy chimed in. "It's always the series ones."

"She'd know, she's dating an accountant!" Nodding, Bailey laughed. "Her man formats pie charts for fun."

"That man also folds fitted sheets like they're origami," Candy said proudly. "We all bring something to the table."

Taylor tried to bite back a smile.

"Alright, but can we talk about how you two looked at each other today?" Candy said, waggling her brows. "It was giving tension. Romance with an invitation for discovery."

"What the hell, Candy? You're watching too many legal dramas." Taylor groaned. "It was not."

Bailey tilted her head and sipped her tea slowly, too slowly. "I've seen that man run cold for decades. He's looking hot. He's definitely into you."

"I think he's just...intense."

Bailey lifted an eyebrow.

"Oh, honey," Candy said, sipping from her mimosa. "I bet he's really good at oral...arguments."

Across from her, Molly sorted swatches of fabric. "He's impressive. Efficient. Takes his time."

"Translation," Bailey said, "Enthusiastic and teachable."

Molly replied, calm as ever. "I have some experience with playing where you work. It's a risky game. He's still your lawyer. Don't let good manners and sweet eyes lure you into mixing business with pleasure."

Taylor flushed. "Signing papers and strategy sessions over coffee aren't a pleasure."

Candy gasped. "Wait. Is he already sending coffee invitations?"

Bailey raised a brow.

"Read it!" Candy pleaded, "Make sure to use your serious courtroom voice."

Taylor rolled her eyes, unlocked her phone, and, with exaggerated formality, read: "Hey. Checking in...You are making sure to get an NDA signed by everyone, right? Say nothing until they've signed one. Bailey said everyone's headed back to Serenity tomorrow. I'm here if you need me. I have some time on Friday if you're free for coffee. Strategy session, of course. Clinton."

"Of course! He wants to discuss strategy." Candy flopped back in her chair and winked.

Taylor groaned and buried her face in her hands. "Why does everything sound flirty when you say it?"

"Because," Candy said, absolutely delighted, "I'm a hopeless romantic."

"Maybe it really is just professional." Taylor tried to keep the tremble from her voice, but the glint in Bailey's eyes told her she wasn't buying it.

"Sure," Molly said dryly. "But also make sure your contract has a clause for when this goes wrong."

Bailey leaned forward, elbows on knees, amusement softening into something deeper. "Jokes aside? I've known Clinton for years. Since Rosie was in diapers and Ethan was giving me migraines. He's overly formal, lives by the law, and once filed a zoning brief while on IV fluids for the flu. He's also kind, steady, and generous, even when people are watching. He knows who he is, and he's fiercely loyal to those he believes in."

She paused, studying Taylor closely. "He's helped me through the worst and never made me apologize. I tease him because someone has to make that man smile more than twice a month, but he's family, and if he sees something in you? If that man wants to be in your corner, don't brush that off."

Taylor blinked, unsure what to say.

"Besides," Bailey added with a gesture at the woman sitting around the room, "They've all found love. Now it's your turn. Candy's busy redecorating the loft with Lincoln manning his spreadsheets. Molly's got Jackson and a baby on the way. Me? I've got Mac, Rosie, and a goat who thinks he's my third child."

"That goat is deeply committed to chaos," Candy agreed.

She leaned closer, speaking gentler. "But Taylor? You've been hiding. For years. First from LA. Then from fashion. Even from your own name. If someone makes you feel seen again? That matters."

Taylor's eyes prickled, but she didn't try to blink it away.

Her phone buzzed again. She glanced down.

Another text from Clinton.

No pressure to decide. Just didn't want you to feel alone.

His vulnerability made her pause, and she continued to delay a response, but her fingers hovered above the keyboard.

"Strategy meeting?" Bailey teased.

Taylor smiled slowly. "Maybe."

Molly raised her glass. "And maybe...it'll just be coffee."

Candy clinked glasses with her. "Or a whole new chance at love."

Bailey grinned. "Or just your turn."

Taylor toasted her champagne glass to the ceiling. "To showing up...regardless of the maybes."

Molly, Bailey, and Candy all clinked in, murmuring variations of amen and hell yes.

Taylor looked down at her phone and started to type a response.

Sure, coffee sounds lovely. Sorry for the long reply; I'm hashing it out and saying goodbye to the girls.

She watched as the three little dots blinked on the screen. It stopped and started flashing again.

Watch Bailey and her scheming; there's only so much I'm legally allowed to do.

She smiled.

I'll text you tomorrow. We'll make plans.

Taylor read it twice, then set her phone down and exhaled.

Maybe it really was just coffee. Perhaps it wasn't.

Chapter Six

Taylor

"Surprise!" exploded in a joyful chorus as Taylor rounded the corner in her flannel pajama pants, clutching a mug of tea, mascara already smudged beneath her eyes. She froze in the kitchen doorway, blinking at the ridiculous parade of her best friends crammed around Bailey's loft table, which was groaning under a tower of pink-frosted cupcakes, disco candles, and a banner pieced together from metallic gift wrap that read: *HAPPY BIRTHDAY, TAYLOR.*

"What—? Oh my God!" she squeaked, trying not to spill hot tea on her pajamas.

Candy sashayed forward balancing a cake wreathed in mint sprigs and sparklers, hollering, "We never got to officially celebrate your birthday! So here's to your big three-oh, babe."

Molly popped a party cracker with a surprisingly robust snap, confetti raining over the countertop. "It's only downhill from here," she intoned, deadpan. "Best get your kicks before your hips start making weather predictions."

Taylor rolled her eyes, laughing as Bailey elbowed Molly with an exaggerated gasp. "Please. My thirties have been the opposite of downhill. I found a handsome man, a career that doesn't feel like I'm drowning, and the best friends a girl could ever want to bury a body with."

"Seconded," Candy sang, spinning the cake so the candles flickered dangerously close to Taylor's nose. "Make a wish!"

Taylor paused, seeing them all in the warm, mismatched glow. Bailey's unruly hair swept up in a glitter scrunchie, Molly perched on the armrest in fuzzy socks and diamonds, Candy practically vibrating with glee. For half a second, she let herself hover in that feeling.

"Blow them out, but don't set your eyebrows on fire," Bailey stage-whispered.

Taylor snorted. "No promises." She closed her eyes, wished for courage, and sent the tiny flames fluttering out. *Maybe her birthday wish would come true.*

Candy immediately started a round of "For She's a Jolly Good Seamstress," and the room broke into off-key singing and cackling. Molly air-drummed; Bailey harmonized with a spoon. When Taylor tried to cover her face with her hands, Bailey snatched them away and linked their fingers. "No hiding, Rousseau. Not tonight."

They squeezed around the crooked kitchen table, plates heaped with cake and mocktails poured into wineglasses for no reason other than the clink.

"You know," Bailey said after a strawberry-sugar bite, "I tried to get you a stripper as a joke, but the agency hung up on me when I specified business casual and a knack for hula hooping in gray sweatpants."

Candy gasped. "Missed opportunity! Lincoln gave me some advice on the best way to fold breakaway pants."

"I don't even want to know." Bailey shivered. "Well, maybe—"

"Nope" Taylor nodded.

"Can you imagine Clinton as a stripper?" Molly deadpanned, eyebrows arching. "He'd itemize every piece of clothing as he removed it."

Taylor snorted tea, sputtering as Candy howled.

"Point is," Bailey said, dabbing at her own mouth, "you deserve the biggest, dumbest celebration for surviving the worst year and leveling up to the best one."

Candy looped her arm around Taylor's shoulders with a conspiratorial grin. "And let's be honest, you need extra well-wishes if you're having coffee with that intimidatingly attractive attorney tomorrow."

"Clinton isn't intimidating," Taylor protested, ears burning. "He's...precise."

"Oh, please." Molly swept her curls over her shoulder. "The way he looks at you is less 'client privilege' and more 'sartorial foreplay.'"

Bailey pointed with her fork. "And he's never asked any of us for coffee after a legal consult. Trust me. He came to my house once. I offered tea, and he left before the steamer even finished."

"He's just—" Taylor started, but Candy shushed her with the dramatic authority of a reality show judge.

"He's temptation walking in a tailored suit, Tay. Own it."

Bailey snickered and propped her chin on her fist, voice

dipping into seriousness between bouts of laughter. "Honestly, though, I've never seen you more...you. Since you started this whole insane New York adventure, you glow differently. Like you realized you don't have to be small to fit in Serenity...or anywhere else."

A hush rippled, soft and easy.

Molly reached across the table to squeeze Taylor's wrist. "It's just nice to see you let someone—him, us, anyone—take care of you a little."

For a moment, Taylor swallowed all the words her friends had handed her. It tasted like home. When she looked up, the love in the room shimmered right through her.

"I can't be small around you three," Taylor said, barely managing not to get teary. "Thanks for making me big again."

Bailey nudged her gently. "Repeat after me. 'I am irreplaceable, and if Bailey starts crying, it's because someone sliced onions for these mocktails.'"

The laughter was instant. With ridiculous ritual, they toasted leftover crumbs instead of glasses, then Candy held up her fork. "To dreams come true, birthday girls with main character energy, and lawyers whose jazz playlists are probably marked 'Confidential.'"

They howled, raising their forks in one last, raucous toast. Laughter spilled and lingered, but soon voices softened to the comfortable hush of friendship winding down.

They wandered to the guest room. All three of them collapsed onto the piled-up blankets, their voices growing drowsy as they planned for morning rideshares and breakfast.

After the lights clicked off, Taylor lay awake in the darkness, listening to her friends breathe. Safe, still surrounded by warmth, she let the feeling linger.

Tomorrow, there would be cars to catch, coffee to pour, another round of hugs and "text us when you land." But tonight, she didn't have to say goodbye. They were all exactly where they belonged—together for one more night, even as the city slowed outside their window.

Chapter Seven

Clinton

"Be careful, it's hot."

Clinton smiled and thanked the server as she placed his cup of black drip coffee on the table.

He'd arrived at the corner café ten minutes early. He was curious if Taylor would be there early, too, but the slight twang of satisfaction he felt confirmed he was right. She was more like the type to be ten minutes late.

"That's fine," he said to himself. He adjusted his cufflinks without thinking, mentally scanning the bullet points he'd prepared for Taylor. NDAs—done. Trademark advisory—outlined. Portfolio archiving—already filed. Check. Check. When he looked into her eyes, he noticed how she was holding up. He knew the case wasn't what had his shoulders tense and his pulse a little too quick.

He was a man of honesty, and he could admit to himself that he wasn't here because of paperwork.

The café was stylish without trying too hard, all muted

wood tones and Edison bulbs, filled with the soft murmur of well-dressed patrons pretending not to eavesdrop. Hidden speakers piped in jazz that made grown men linger over their espresso as if they could time-travel through taste.

Clinton picked the place for its privacy. The booths were deep, and the angles weren't intimidating. It also helped that the barista recognized his order immediately. Despite his polished exterior, Clinton valued simplicity. Taylor, on the other hand, wasn't simple.

He took a seat at the corner booth and slid his tablet onto the table. When the server appeared, he nodded his thanks. "Just the usual, for now, but my companion will want something when she arrives," he said, tapping his pen on the table without looking up.

From the moment Taylor Rousseau walked through the door, the entire café shifted.

He didn't look immediately, not wanting to seem overeager, but he knew. The air changed. He sensed the movement of her and her colors at the peripheral edges.

When he looked up, his eyes found her immediately. She wore high-waisted jeans, a bottle-green jacket that fit like it had been made for her, which it probably had, and a soft cream scarf tucked carelessly around her throat. Hair was pulled up. It wasn't what you'd call messy, but also not quite formal—an artist, even in track lighting.

She scanned the room and found him. Her shoulders squared.

That simple motion—chin up, spine tall—had him sitting straighter in response.

"Ms. Rousseau," he said as she approached, but there was no bite in it.

"Clint," she replied, easing into the seat across from him.

He arched a brow. She smirked.

Their dynamic wasn't what he was used to. It wasn't flirtation, exactly, but there was electricity in it. A current of awareness ran just beneath the surface. Not only was she engaging with him, but she was also challenging him to challenge her back.

"I brought my notes," she said, fishing a slim notepad from her oversized satchel. "Figured if this is a 'strategy session,' I might as well pretend I know what I'm doing."

Clinton allowed himself a small, rare smile. "You're doing more than pretending."

She gave him a look. "It still feels like I'm in someone else's movie."

"Then you've cast yourself well."

Her laugh was soft, uncertain. "You've got lines," she said, echoing Candy's teasing from earlier in the week. "That's dangerous coming from a man who's comfortable standing in a room full of people and being unapologetically right."

"I practiced in the mirror," he deadpanned.

That earned a genuine smile. Her guard ticked down, just a notch, and Clinton realized how much of her resilience was woven right into her posture with her chin lifted, and her shoulders set like they'd been ironed into place. Confidence wasn't a layer she put on. She wore it like armor.

"You don't appear to foster a lack of confidence, either," he said, tone dry but not unkind. "I've never met someone who could make a café booth look like a royal procession. You sit like the seat belongs to you, and always did."

She gave a small snort, amused. "Modeling lessons."

He waited, curious.

She shrugged one shoulder, the movement graceful. "The runway will teach you to stand tall. Even when your underwear's held together with duct tape, your shoes are two sizes too small, and there's a very real chance you're about to trip, flash the front row, or fall both literally and professionally on your face. It doesn't matter. You keep walking. Chin up, eyes straight. Fake the elegance until you believe it yourself."

His brows lifted. "That sounds worse than the LSATs. At least during that test, I knew my clothes wouldn't betray me."

"Oh no," she said, smiling slyly. "The clothing is the least treacherous part. It's the eyes. Everyone's watching, waiting for you to mess up. You learn to control every twitch, every blink. You learn poise like a language."

Clinton nodded slowly, surprisingly thoughtful. "I think I only learned poise from cross-examination prep. Now, I'm wondering how I'd hold up with blistered heels on polished tile and strangers judging the width of my lapel."

She grinned. "Depends on the lapel."

The moment stretched. She looked effortless, but he could see it now. There was an intention behind every movement. The spine behind the silk. The quiet decision to show up anyway, even when everything felt stitched together with doubt.

And he respected the hell out of it.

"It's definitely a skill." Taylor gestured to the tentative outline she'd sketched out. Dates and times were comparing her work against Delacroix, including some sample sketches and pictures she'd clearly printed off the internet. It was intriguing, even if it wasn't definitive.

He ran his finger along her notes, comparing them in his head against his own. He slid the tablet in front of her, guiding their attention to his notes. "There are gaps in the timeline I'd like to see if we can fill. Specifically, between your capstone submission and Delacroix's first public showing."

She nodded, tucking one leg under her. "I'm almost positive I still have an email thread from that semester, where I sent him some early idea roughs and he gave feedback."

Clinton's brows lifted. "You do?"

She nodded. "I didn't think of it until you said something, but I had a 'we might need that' upbringing and tend to hoard things. I'm very resourceful that way, much to the detriment of my storage space."

He chuckled. "Right now, that's exceedingly useful."

The coffees arrived. There was a perfect unsweetened pour for him, and something foamy, fragrant, and topped with cinnamon for her.

She sipped before speaking. "Delacroix used to say real artists were 'above needing credit.' That obsession with recognition was vulgar. It doesn't appear to apply to him. Maybe it's just for women he doesn't want taking up his space."

"You know that's not fair, right? You don't have to give away or let people take things from you." Clinton's tone was quiet, but the edge was there.

Something in her froze when he said that word. Theft. Her fingers curled tightly around the mug.

"I don't know what Laurent Delacroix thinks anymore," she said. "But I remember what I thought then. He was the expert, and I should be grateful for his time and advice. Clearly, they'd all made a mistake admitting a girl who made gowns out of church curtains and stitched poetry into fedora linings."

Clinton swallowed. "You weren't a mistake, Taylor. You were a threat."

She lifted her eyes then, and the way she looked at him...

He knew better than this. Knew not to lean into moments like these. Not with clients. Not with someone this tangled in high emotion and risk, but what she needed now wasn't a lawyer's restraint. It wasn't bullet points and timestamps.

It was a belief.

So, he gave it to her. Gently. Clearly. "That man made a career cannibalizing the hopes of hungry talent. But you? You built something new from scraps. You were never small. He didn't know how to make room for you."

Her throat worked around a swallow, and then she nodded slowly.

They returned to details, pages of timelines and statements to collect. Passwords to old emails she'd sheepishly admit still existed in her inbox, but even as they worked, something changed. He heard it in her voice, as her confidence increased and her certainty hardened. She was easing into the space, slowly reclaiming herself stitch by stitch.

When she stood to leave, an hour later, they lingered by the door too long. She looked up at him—really looked—and he saw something unspoken there. A question he wasn't ready to answer.

Not yet.

But she smiled, and he returned it.

"Thank you," she said quietly, her words brushing against something he didn't want to name.

He wanted to say, "It's my job." It was more personal than that, though. He thought back to his final year at Columbia Law—that strange blur of caffeine-fueled nights and polished confidence. Then, everyone had been experiencing some sort of existential crisis. The imposter syndrome was almost fashionable. They laughed about it over flat whites and case briefs, trading self-deprecating remarks like currency. For most of them, the doubt was temporary. It was something that skimmed the surface and never quite stuck. Their value and their worth were never really tied up in it.

Taylor clearly hadn't had friends, professors, or family to encourage her in the ways she needed. Taylor hadn't had peers questioning her. No cozy study group, comparing LSAT scores, waiting for the pizza delivery guy.

The reminder sparked even more memories that had been pushed back for more than a decade, hints of uncertainty that lingered at the edges that he hadn't thought about in ages. In remembering, another name surfaced. Sara.

She had been the first and the last woman he'd ever loved. Sara, with her cello-shaped curves and soft-spoken charm, had had all the right schools and unlimited resources. On the outside, composed, prim, proper, and always put together in the latest designer clothes. Unlike Taylor, she was dripping with luxury brands that matched her mother's country club's expectations. On the outside, she'd had everything. Helen was precisely the sort of woman you were supposed to build a life with.

Everything was available to her, and when she'd had to take something for herself—start a career, stand in front of a jury and take up space, demand outcomes based on the decisions she'd made—she couldn't hold the weight of performance.

Helen had fallen apart.

She hadn't just doubted herself...she'd drowned in it. The more she tried to hold the image together, the faster it unraveled. A breakdown in a lecture hall, then a three-day psychiatric hold that no one talked about, and a week later, she boarded a plane home to Connecticut and never came back.

He'd tried. Called. Wrote letters. Tried to visit.

But love couldn't fix what someone refused to claim, and, in the end, he'd solved the puzzle. People were unpredictable and often unreliable. It was fine if you expected that, but not great if you were trying to build a life with someone. So, he never had.

He kept work, life, and love separate. Compartmentalized, and that had worked for him. He wasn't ready and knew it was incredibly unwise to let Taylor mess up the life he'd made for himself.

Taylor frightened him with the way she pressed into her purpose and barely allowed herself softness. And in the way, her voice wavered when she was brave. She reminded him of the part of Helen no one saw, only louder, bolder, more courageous, and with more fire behind the hurt. It didn't stop him from worrying if it would all be too much for her, or from thinking she now had resources she hadn't had before.

And he wasn't sure he could survive watching someone unravel again.

So, instead of brushing it off with professional detachment or clinging too tightly to history, Clinton straightened his shoulders, met her gaze, and said, "You're not alone anymore."

Chapter Eight

Taylor

The city was never quiet at night. Even this high above the street, in Bailey's loft, Taylor could still hear the occasional taxi horn or the murmur of sidewalk conversations. Once her friends had gone home, the buzz beneath it all—New York's heartbeat—slowed just enough to let her think.

Which was the problem.

Taylor sat curled on the couch in a worn hoodie swiped from Bailey's guest closet. Her sketchbooks were spread across her lap, fabric swatches fanned out at her side. The pages beneath her fingers brimmed with potential, but her hand wouldn't move.

The overhead lights had long since been turned off. Only the warm glow of an old Tiffany lamp lit the room, casting a rainbow haze across the hardwood.

She breathed deeply. She'd never journaled. Instead, she loved to draw and create the pictures in her head, not talk about or unpack them. It cleared her mind to take her thoughts and filter them through curves and seams and imaginary threads.

So why couldn't she sketch now?

Her fingers hovered above the page. In her mind, clear as if it had just happened, she saw it again. The dress.

The final gown that had stomped down the runway and shattered the quiet life she'd built in Serenity. The same embroidery, the same sleeve scissored into a bell, and the collar—pleated, high-set—a clear nod to the Edwardian renaissance gowns she'd obsessed over in design school.

She reached to her right and flipped open one of her old sketchbooks, which had finally arrived after Max sent them. The pages had yellowed slightly, but the graphite lines still held their shape. Decisive strokes. A smudged name printed on the cover in her mother's handwriting: Taylor Rousseau.

She smiled faintly.

There was something sacred about these pages. Within these pages, she'd illustrated her dreams before she was told her instincts were "frivolous" and her originality "naïve."

She traced the sketchbook spine. The paper was softened by years and humidity. There was the page filled with tiny gowns she'd scribbled while riding the metro. The half-sketched coat, imagined while freezing beside the radiator in her first shoebox apartment. Most of these designs had never seen the light of day—not even Delacroix had seen them. But the ones she'd photographed with her cracked iPhone? The ones she'd uploaded to the mentor forum during her final semester.

She knew he'd seen those.

Taylor clicked open a hidden folder on her tablet, bracing herself as thumbnails bloomed across the screen—years of his collections, downloaded in quiet acts of self-torture. She'd never let herself look too closely. Never zoomed. Never read the descriptions that praised innovation that wasn't his to claim.

But now?

Now she couldn't afford not to.

She took a shaky breath and opened another tab, pulling up a Delacroix collection from two years ago. There. The oceanic blue train. Her train. The one she'd draped to mimic deep waves after dreaming of her mother's old photos from Galveston—the ones that had lived on their fridge as coastal reminders in their landlocked kitchen.

She clicked on the runway interview. A video clip from an Italian fashion site played—subtitles flickering beneath Delacroix's smug face.

"Where did the inspiration come from?" the host had asked.

"The sea," he said smoothly. "The sea is an endless source of mystery and challenge—ever-changing, ever-demanding. Fashion must be the same."

Taylor paused the clip. Dragged open her scanned sketch.

There it was. Not inspired. Not revised. Stolen. The lines were identical—down to the tucked curl at the collar and the asymmetry along the hem.

Taylor blinked hard, a stinging tightness flaring behind her eyes. Her lungs caught mid-breath, like her own body couldn't believe what it was seeing. She leaned closer to the screen, pulse fluttering. Her hand hovered, suspended in doubt, and then moved—hesitant, then desperate for proof.

Another design. And another.

A fitted blue silk bodice with organza sleeves that dripped like wax—hers.

A three-tiered tulle skirt pleated into roses at the hip-bone—hers.

A belted kimono jacket with silk-screened peonies—hers.

Each one sharpened the ache in her chest until it bloomed into something far deeper than outrage. It wasn't just anger twisting in her gut. It was betrayal. Sorrow. A deep, raw mourning for the girl she had been when she first dreamed these designs—the girl who hadn't known how to armor herself, yet. The girl who thought talent was enough. Who'd walked into that mentorship believing she'd finally been seen.

Her fingers moved faster now, breath shallow, shoulders curving inward like she could shrink from the blow. But there was no escaping it. Image after image flashed across the screen. There was no denying it anymore. He'd taken the designs and inspirations of her work—without hesitation, without shame—and paraded them for the world with his name sewn into every boldfaced headline and printed program.

A sound escaped her—short, low, guttural. It took a second for her to realize it had come from her own throat. Something between grief and fury, grief and guilt.

A memory surfaced uninvited: herself, years younger, eyes red and raw after another day of juggling her work, her school, and her life. She'd bolstered herself by pretending in the mirror that she was being interviewed. Imagining what it would feel like to share her work. To have built something worthy of all her hard work.

She had whispered thank-yous to invisible audiences back

then. Rehearsed what she would say. How she might describe the feeling of creation.

Except now those interviews existed—and they didn't belong to her. Her younger self had imagined glory; Taylor now watched that fantasy handed to someone else who might have once earned it, but now kept his illustrious fame by cheating and stealing.

Her jaw trembled. Not with rage. With empathy. With heartbreak.

For the girl on the studio floor in nothing but day-old mascara and a hem stuck halfway to finished, whispering her future into the fabric and hoping it would hear her.

She deserved better.

Taylor's spine curled forward and her arms wrapped around her ribs—tight. Her whole body ached in strange and specific places, like every image struck just below the skin. Behind her sternum. Deep in her hips. Between her shoulder blades, where tension from a thousand bent hours still remembered the posture of hope.

She opened a spreadsheet. Familiar, decisive motions. Needed structure, a place to stack the pain.

Her hands moved with mechanical precision. Sketch title. Date submitted. Forum upload. Delacroix debut. Collection name. Motif. Material. The clack of keys sounded like a metronome marking the beat of resilience.

She began color-coding the ones that matched too closely.

A pale pink sketch faded behind her spreadsheet window as she typed:

Original submission: March 8. Upload: March 22.

Delacroix debut: Paris Fashion Week—September, same year.

All that time, her silence had resulted in consent. Not intentional—but no less effective. That silence had cost her everything.

Behind her, the fireplace crackled like applause she didn't deserve. Her boutique in Serenity had given her a taste of what she loved—something to hold on to—but it had pulled her away from her real dreams, just as effectively as Delacroix's hateful final words.

Not until that fateful day on the runway...not until Mystique was born...had she felt anything other than resignation and remorse.

Her notes took shape across the screen: Twenty-three original sketches. Seventeen copied nearly line for line across a variety of collection. Six adjusted—minimally.

A few hemlines and stitches changed here and there, like he'd been correcting her work across time and distance.

Taylor laid her palm flat on the scanned sketchbook page. "You dressed dreams," she whispered. Then louder: "And you still do."

Taylor opened the file with the dress. The one that had walked the runway under someone else's name.

With steady hands, she began uploading the documentation into a secure folder for Clinton. Every file labeled. Tagged. Dated. Organized.

She didn't care how quietly they had to start. Or how slowly they'd build momentum.

Piece by piece, she was taking it back.

When she was done—when every sketch was scanned,

zipped, encrypted, and backed up twice—she exhaled.

The hum of Bailey's old side table lamp joined the quiet pulse of the city outside as she pulled a blank sketchpad toward her and stared at the page. Designing used to be as simple as breathing, but she'd restrained the ideas for so long, they felt locked up inside her.

She didn't dive in with old designs. This time, she waited—knees folded, eyes closed—and listened for what was still inside her.

Then her pencil moved.

Not runway flair or trend-chasing poses. These were shapes that felt real: A palazzo silhouette with a waterfall hem, pleated vertically for ease and elegance. A wrap dress with an exaggerated sash and secret pockets. A blazer-dress hybrid, sculpted with curves instead of corners.

Soft. Certain. Structural but not strict. Delicate without apology.

The kind of clothes a woman wore when she didn't need her outfit to speak for her—but loved when it did.

Three full pages poured out before she paused for her forgotten tea. It was cold. She didn't care.

The pencil shifted again.

A sleeve that collapsed like a blooming flower. A hem that dipped low in the back, but stayed high in front—a contradiction by design. A modular shift gown with weighted panels and adjustable seams.

She blinked and smiled.

These hadn't lived in Milan. Or LA. Or even in her younger dreams, back when she'd been inspired by lanky models and professors who droned on about concept over connection.

They were new.

They were hers.

By the time the first rays of light crept through the tall windows, Taylor's back ached, her jaw was sore, and her fingers were stained with charcoal and ink.

The teacup was empty.

The sketches were everywhere.

And still—she smiled. Not the brittle kind she used to fake through fear.

But the soft, slow kind. Because somewhere between uploading her past and inviting it to stay exactly where it belonged—behind her—she'd discovered the next version of herself.

Chapter Nine

Taylor

The elevator doors opened onto the twelfth floor of the Ladder H headquarters. Sunlight poured across polished concrete, catching on steel beams and the rows of tall windows. The space stretched wide and spare, not flashy, but ready to be claimed.

Bailey walked ahead, boots clicking with purpose. "This floor normally sits empty after Q3," she said, motioning toward the long bank of windows. "West light until dinner, reliable plumbing, and a freight elevator that actually works. You'll thank me when the fabric shipments come in."

Taylor followed, taking in the garment racks already lined up against the wall, folding tables stacked with bolts of silk and organza, and a humming espresso machine waiting in the corner. It looked less like an office floor than a workshop mid-transformation.

Bailey glanced back at her. "I had my assistant put out a call for temp seamstresses. You've got five on-site today. They've all got NDAs signed, and they're all vetted. Our IT set you up with security fobs. No one enters unless they're rostered to Mystique or you personally call them. We clear at six so the cleaners can do their thing at night."

Taylor's throat tightened. "Bailey, this…this is beyond generous. I can't believe you'd risk turning your headquarters into Project Runway, Underground Edition."

"You ran from LA with two suitcases and built a boutique out of duct tape and hope. Investing in you isn't a risk. It's stupid not to." Bailey's smile softened but stayed sure. "You've already proved you can build something from scratch. This time, you'll have tools instead of obstacles."

Before she could muster a reply, phones pinged. A text from Molly popped up: *Make the front desk sign for the specialty thread delivery. I don't want stock accidentally going home with someone's cousin.*

Candy chimed in two seconds later: *Expect a cupcake delivery. You can bribe the UPS guy, and I want pictures.*

Bailey smirked. "Classic. Molly policing deliveries, Candy bribing you with sugar."

Footsteps sounded in the entryway. Clinton appeared, briefcase in hand, gaze sweeping across the fabric, machines, and post-it-covered bulletin boards. "So this is what fast-tracking production looks like."

His eyes landed on Taylor, steady, weighing.

Bailey crossed her arms. "Here to drown us in paperwork, or just to make it look official?"

Clinton handed her a folder. "Partnership addendum. Building use, liability, equipment insurance. Straightforward. Review before signing."

Bailey slid it onto a rack without looking. "If he sounds bossy, it's because he thinks ahead. Don't worry. He's helpful even when he's not quoting contracts."

Taylor shifted. "You think we're pushing too hard?"

Clinton's reply was gentle but honest. "I think you're scaling at warp speed, but you're smart, and you have a team that loves you enough to lose sleep. I also think the next twenty-four hours are everything. Don't trust the city to forgive mistakes."

For a split second, Taylor bristle. Was he worried about her, or did he not believe she could handle it?

But Clinton stepped closer, his serious mask cracking just enough. "You don't need warnings, Taylor. You need backup. I came to see if you wanted an extra set of hands, or someone to handle dinner."

Bailey lifted a brow. "Or someone to remind the temps that yes, Taylor's in charge."

Taylor let the tension ease. "I do need backup," she said, looking at Clinton. "And I could use someone who knows how to spot a fire before it starts."

He gave her a rare smile. "Then I'll get takeout and make rounds. Maybe even lend a hand with quality control, if you trust me near a needle."

Taylor's grin returned. "Not a chance."

Laughter rippled between them as the seamstresses returned to their machines. Bailey slung an arm around Taylor's shoulders. "You're in it now, and you're not in it alone."

Chapter Ten

Taylor

Taylor woke to the sound of her phone buzzing insistently against the couch cushion. Pale mid-morning sunlight bled through the gauzy curtains of Bailey's loft, warming her cheek where she'd collapsed hours earlier.

She sat up slowly, her spine protesting, and blinked at the screen.

A text from Clinton.

Please don't read it alone.

That was it. No signature. No flourish.

She stared at it, heart thumping harder than it had any right to for a four-word message. She looked around the room, but being alone wasn't as simple as usual.

Her fingers hovered, then tapped the link he'd sent. A New York Times Style headline appeared across the screen: *Laurent Delacroix: Fashion's Unmatched Genius.*

Beneath the opulent, serif-font title was a familiar byline, followed by a curated gallery of images from last weekend's show, with each one drawing praise.

She scrolled numbly through each photo, her stomach twisting.

There it was—a picture of the final look. Her look. Center stage. On a model wearing the pleated butterfly collar, she had once taken a shot under the flickering light of a borrowed desk lamp. The quote for the article hung at the top in bold: "Delacroix dares to lend a softness to fashion that nurtures unapologetic femininity."

She liked the line. She hated handing her praise to Delacroix.

The paragraph scrolled under her thumb, and she skimmed the text. The review praised the collection as "a return to peak Delacroix, full of designs that ache with history and heart."

A bitter laugh slipped from her lips.

Taylor stood too quickly, ignoring the paper skidding to the floor, and shaking out her limbs still heavy with sleep. She stumbled toward the kitchen for water she didn't really want, then called Clinton.

He answered on the second ring. "Taylor?"

"I should've waited," she said. "I'm sorry."

"No apology needed," he replied, voice pitched calm and low. She imagined him in his office already, with his tie straight, mug full, and laptop humming.

"It's just...I had trouble sleeping last night. When I woke up to your message, I couldn't help but know."

She heard the rustle of paper at his end and wondered if he was skimming a copy of the Times.

"He's digging in," Clinton said. "Claiming the show as a

return to his roots. Leaning into nostalgia as a design philosophy."

"He's leaning into my nostalgia," she muttered.

Clinton paused. "This is working." The line went silent. Then he said, "He's worried."

Taylor sat on the floor beside Bailey's coffee table, curling her knees to her chest. "Why do you think that?"

"Because," Clinton said, "he's leading with interviews and sentiment instead of exclusivity. Laurent Delacroix doesn't do public. He doesn't explain, and now he's scrambling to protect a narrative."

She picked at a frayed thread on her cuff. "So, what do we do?"

"You decide," Clinton said. "We can go forward full throttle. File the initial letter with the IP counsel and draft a formal statement. We shift from silence to strategy and start making your presence known, or..." his voice softened, "we wait. Keep feeding Mystique. Let the buzz keep rising."

"IP?"

"Sorry, Intellectual Property."

"What would you do?" she asked.

"I'm not you," he replied gently. "You've got to live with the consequences, not me."

Taylor stared at the pile of sketches strewn across the floor and the list she'd made overnight. It was filled with names, dates, and the lineage of every design.

She thought about Bailey. About Serenity, and the quiet charm of her boutique. About her mom's endless encouragement. She thought about the words she used to stitch into her linings: *For you. Not for the world.*

"Hold off on filing the paperwork. I want to give the Mystique line time to get traction. I also want to discuss the historical use timeline with you."

What she didn't want to say was: *I'm not ready to face him yet.*

Three hours later, Taylor was still barefoot in Bailey's loft, hunched on the floor with her hair looped into a messy braid and black graphite smudged across two fingers and one cheekbone. The sketches were piled up around her hips, and a swath of charmeuse silk swatches fanned out beneath her thighs.

Her phone buzzed beside a half-finished mug of tea. Bailey.

Taylor answered and didn't even get out a hello before her best friend's voice burst through with the enthusiasm of someone who'd had three strong coffees and a victory to report.

"Okay, listen!" Bailey's voice crackled with glee. "Did you see the Fashion Weekly article? The quote about the shadow designer with a signature silhouette that's rumored to be reinventing New York runways?"

Taylor blinked, a little dazed. "No? I've been...uh...sketching."

"Well, they're talking about you," Bailey said smugly. "I also sent Clinton a PDF to document your involvement and ensure we're protecting the brand."

"I talked to him this morning," Taylor murmured. "After the New York Times article."

Bailey went quiet on the other end for just a beat. "Yeah. I saw that."

Skipping past the feelings she'd already spent all day feeling, she kept moving forward. "He and I talked about the sketches and the comparisons. I started organizing everything. I put it all in the shared drive he set up."

"And?" Bailey asked, too casually.

"And he said we have a case," Taylor whispered. "It's not formally filed, but he's setting up preliminary protections. I'm giving him the originals this week."

Bailey let out a gentle, impressed exhale. "Rousseau, you sneaky little powerhouse."

"I'm not trying to make a scene," Taylor murmured, brushing hair from her face. "I just...want the truth to outlast the PR hype."

"Oh, the PR is doing just fine," Bailey chirped. "Molly worked her press magic yesterday. I gave her full creative range, and she built out a rollout that's impossible to ignore. We've got whisper campaigns running from SoHo boutiques to Tribeca stylists, and Candy? God bless her sweet, chaotic soul. She overnighted cupcakes to every New York fashion Influencer under thirty-five."

"Not that half of them even eat cupcakes." Taylor covered her eyes with one hand, laughing. "You're insane."

"Insanely effective," Bailey corrected. "Also, two more clients reached out to schedule fittings this morning. Gita Sheng's stylist called personally and said the coat Mystique designed made her cry. Vivienne Chen's assistant asked for a rush order."

"Wait. Vivienne Chen? Like…the editor emeritus of Luxe?"

"The one and only. She changed her bio pic on the fashion council site to a blurry screenshot of your gown and sent a group text to twelve buyers with money sign emojis. Which, I believe, constitutes approval."

Taylor's jaw dropped.

Bailey continued without pause. "Oh, and by the way? We're auctioning off one of your dresses."

Taylor blinked hard. "We're what?"

Bailey grinned audibly through the phone. "The Pour with Purpose Gala. It's Ladder H's annual fundraiser, and this year it's benefiting youth arts education and creative equity. Think champagne, high society, too many men with cravats. It's two weeks out, we've got major media lined up. We've historically auctioned off exclusive bottles, heirloom jewelry, and a rare bourbon last year, but this year? We're auctioning off a Mystique original."

A beat of silence followed.

"A rare original we don't have, yet," said Taylor, but she sat up straighter. "You really think people will bid on it?"

Bailey snorted. "Honey, they're already asking where to sign up. The buzz is real, and you're still anonymous. That's half the appeal. We're dressing a few select women in advance, but the gala gown? That's a one-of-a-kind, no-replicas-ever piece. It'll walk the carpet once and belong to the highest bidder. Dripping with Mystique magic."

Taylor laughed through her disbelief. "You're all in on this mystery woman thing, aren't you?"

"Taylor," Bailey said, and her voice turned unexpectedly

gentle. "You've been hiding for so long, but right now? The industry is on fire, trying to figure out who you are, and instead of letting fear shut it all down, you're rising. Don't flinch now."

"I'm making things. Real things. Not knockoffs, edits, or timid spins. They're mine this time." Taylor swallowed. "I'm going to need help from one or a dozen seamstresses. I can't sew this fast!"

"We'll figure it out quickly. It's about hiring and NDAs, so we can assign Clinton's team to it," Bailey said, proud and composed. "And we're not just reclaiming a story, we're shaping a future. One dress at a time." Then, with a grin clearly visible even through a phone line, she added, "Now, grab yourself a snack and put on lipstick or pajamas. I don't care which. You'll want to feel like a million bucks while you invest in your creative greatness."

Taylor laughed, full and quiet. "Speaking of invest…"

"Meh, Clinton's got that covered. You probably didn't notice, but while your handsome attorney had you signing all those papers, you picked up a silent investor."

"I'm going to make it worth every penny."

Bailey paused, letting the moment land with the importance it deserved. "Never doubted that."

They hung up.

Taylor leaned back against the couch, letting the moment settle over her. As crazy as it felt, their wild plan might actually work.

Chapter Eleven

Clinton

The Met was crowded on a Saturday afternoon with photographers, parents pushing strollers, and students who loitered in their curated shade of intellectual chic. Clinton Conners usually felt at home here, among the polished marble, the hushed reverence of art lovers, and overpriced gift-shop wares.

But today, he was anxiously scanning the entrance steps for a woman with the disarming habit of making him forget he'd once sworn never to mix the personal with the professional ever again.

Taylor Rousseau moved through the sidewalk crowds as if parting the Red Sea. She wore all-black cropped trousers, a satiny wrap-style blouse that dipped at the collar, and a wool trench casually over one arm. Practical boots. Oversized sunglasses. She looked effortless. Controlled.

People moved aside for her.

"Clint," she greeted, pushing her sunglasses into her hair.

"Clinton," he replied automatically, but softened the edge

with a nod. "You're on time."

Taylor shrugged. "Figured I'd ruin your expectations early. Can't have you assuming I'm a disorganized artist a second time."

"You're not disorganized," he said. "You're easily inspired. There's a difference."

That earned him a smile. Not the tight one he'd seen her use to appear in control, but the one that surfaced right before she did something bold.

He'd never liked surprises, but he was looking forward to the ones she brought.

"Thank you for joining me today. I thought you might enjoy seeing more of New York since Bailey isn't around much." He didn't add that he'd been worried about her since the Delacroix headlines had dropped.

"Of course. Thank you for inviting me."

Clinton glanced around. "Any artist worth their title has been to the Met. You can't visit New York without making at least a quick trip to soak in the inspiration."

He also didn't admit he'd been looking for an excuse to see her again, and she didn't seem inclined to call him out on his poorly concealed attempt to impress her.

They walked beneath the museum's grand columns together. He'd reserved timed passes to the Modern and Contemporary floor as an excuse to talk art, not law—her territory.

At first, they said little. Rows of visitors flowed around them, and the museum pulsed softly with footfalls and murmured conversations. The occasional tour guide's voice drifted past.

Clinton kept his hands tucked in the pockets of his trousers, his gaze lingering on bold sweeps of color and deliberate lines, but his attention kept tilting sideways and watching her more than the art.

Taylor's arms folded loosely across her middle. Her posture held an architecture he was starting to recognize. *Grace shaped by grit.* She didn't fidget. Didn't fill the silence. She just stood there, letting it speak for her.

To most onlookers, they would seem like two professionals out for a casual stroll, pausing before abstract lines and negative space, but to each other? Every heartbeat felt like a fresh recalibration. That charged hum that lives beneath shared quiet.

"She was one of my first favorites," Taylor said as they paused before a Lee Krasner piece. The splattered chaos still managed direction, but along with something primal and honest.

"She?" Clinton asked.

"Lee. Jackson Pollock's wife."

He turned slightly. "You like the abstract expressionists?"

"I like the ones who surprised people." Taylor tilted her head. "Even when she was married to someone louder, people eventually saw her for herself. It just...took twice as long."

"I imagine that's familiar."

She didn't flinch. "Not just in fashion. Everywhere."

Their steps echoed as they continued. When they reached the Mondrian, he slowed. She did too. Their pace shifted into lockstep.

"He simplifies everything into geometry," he said, watching her.

"I don't think so," Taylor replied. "He elevates simplicity. Reduces the noise but keeps the soul. That's the difference."

He glanced down at her. Her expression was thoughtful, not just admiring the art, but folding herself into it.

"That's what you do," he said, without thinking.

She turned. "Excuse me?"

"You reduce complications without losing feeling. Your sketches are emotional without being indulgent. They carry structure. Intent."

Her brows lifted. "A compliment? From Clinton Conners? Be still, my creative heart."

"I parse my compliments carefully."

"You ration emotions."

He liked her like this. She was sharp, not shielded. Emboldened. It made it easier to pretend it didn't matter that her laugh kept landing somewhere behind his collarbone.

They wandered into a quiet side gallery brimming with lesser-known Impressionists.

"Did you always want to be a lawyer?" She asked as they slowed between paintings. "Was that the dream?"

"No," he answered honestly. "But it was the safest option for someone in my family who liked puzzles more than people."

"That sounds depressing," she said, head tilted.

"Not when you make it a skill. I pursued precision, control, and guarantees."

"And I pursued whimsy and silk appliqué." She smiled faintly. "Attraction of opposites, I suppose."

He looked at her. "Attraction?"

Her lips parted slightly. "No?"

Clinton hesitated. "An ill-advised attraction."

That quieted her. Not because of shame, but because naming things made them too real.

They paused beside a Lucian Freud sketch. A study of a female back, undone, but not vulnerable. Observed, not stolen.

Clinton studied it for a beat.

"Are you ever afraid," he asked quietly, "that you won't be able to carry what comes next?"

Taylor didn't answer immediately. "You mean success?"

"I mean anything. After this exposure. Win or lose, when it's all in full transparency...does that scare you?"

She stood still.

"Sometimes," she admitted. "But more than fear, I feel... hungry. Like I've been starving for attention, and that terrifies me."

"That you'll chase it?"

"No, that I'll lose myself to it," she said. "That I'll fall to the same temptations as Delacroix. That I'll stop creating to make people feel better and start creating to make myself feel better."

He studied her, the set of her jaw, the twist of her fingers in her pocket.

"I've seen people give everything they had to a dream," he said, stepping closer. It wasn't enough to touch, but enough to breathe her in. "And I've watched what happens when the scaffolding gives out. I don't sign people up for loss, Taylor. I don't gamble on futures to make a point."

She turned toward him, the shift in her expression soft and startled, like she'd seen something in him he hadn't meant to show. Her gaze was steady. Curious. Open.

He remembered that gaze, or one like it.

Helen had once looked at him that way from a lawn chair with bare feet tucked beneath her, a law school outline in one hand, and a textbook on her knee. She'd said she was going to change the world. When the cracks came and the floor gave out, she'd broken too fast and too quietly for anyone to stop it.

Her self-worth had been wrapped too tightly in being chosen, respected, and admired. When she wasn't...it all unraveled.

He'd held the pieces or tried to.

Ambition, he'd learned, cuts both ways. It can build someone up bright-eyed and burning, but it can also hollow them out when the world fails to meet their expectations.

But Taylor wasn't Sara.

Her ambition wasn't for applause. It was for ownership. She didn't chase validation. She craved proof. Still, Clinton saw the flicker of danger. It was a pull, not just to take part in the world, but to reshape it.

His jaw flexed. "I just need to know you'll have something solid when the glitter fades, when the proof is on paper, and reality comes to rest. Not everyone does."

After a moment, she asked quietly, "Do you think I'll fall apart?"

"That's not it." His voice softened. "I think you're building something beautiful. I want to make sure you don't burn it down chasing approval you don't need."

A beat passed.

Then she asked, "Are you counting this toward your billable hours?"

Clinton's mouth twitched. "I have in the past, but this

time? I appear to have a much more personal motive."

"Lucky me," she murmured.

They finished the exhibit slowly, walking back into the gentle bustle of the main floor. Outside, the light had shifted when they descended the marble steps.

"I'm starving," she said.

"There are food vendors in the park."

Her brows lifted. "You mean…a food truck?"

"I mean, avoiding mustard stains on my tie while eating a street pretzel next to a woman whose fashion sense intimidates half of Manhattan." He gestured to her outfit. "That's not dry clean only, is it?"

Her smile was sudden and soft. "Now, that's how to woo a girl."

Ten minutes later, they stood shoulder-to-shoulder in front of a bustling halal cart on the edge of the park, the air thick with cinnamon-spiced steam and chili-charred smoke.

Taylor leaned slightly forward, squinting at the menu. "Okay. I'm torn between the lamb gyro and the falafel plate. I feel like they both say, 'I'm a woman of complex tastes and powerful ankle boots.'"

Clinton didn't look up from the menu. "They both also say, 'messy lunch on important paperwork.'"

"You wound me, Counselor," she said, faux aghast. "You didn't even glance at my boots."

Clinton allowed himself the briefest glance—ankle-grazing black leather, zippered, and sculpted like they meant business. "Impressive. Tactical footwear. I assume they double as a weapon?"

"If by 'weapon' you mean crushing my enemies beneath the heel of precise tailoring, then yes."

The man behind the cart tapped his spatula on the grill. "You two dating or fighting?"

Taylor smiled. "Is there a difference?"

Clinton lifted a brow. "We'll take a lamb gyro and one spicy bratwurst, and two iced teas."

"Hot sauce?" the vendor asked.

"No for me," Taylor said, raising a hand. "I don't need drama."

"Absolutely yes," Clinton said. "I thrive under pressure."

Taylor side-eyed him. "That explains the pocket square flourish."

The vendor chuckled as he handed them their food. They strolled toward the nearest shaded bench, dodging pigeons and small children with sticky fingers until they found a spot flanked by a vendor selling knockoff sunglasses and an older man feeding birds who looked like he hadn't moved from his spot since Nixon.

Clinton unbuttoned his jacket before sitting, making a small show of delicately folding it over the back of the bench.

"Of course you don't eat spicy sausage in a blazer," Taylor whispered around a bite. "Even your street food manners wear cufflinks."

He glanced down to find her balancing her gyro across a sketchpad in her lap as an improvised picnic plate, tzatziki dripping precariously close to a sleeve sketch.

"You're getting sauce on your fashion legacy."

"I'm a professional artist," she said, unbothered.

Clinton shook his head, smirking as he took a bite. His brow furrowed in surprise. "This bratwurst is excellent. Unexpectedly spicy."

Tucking her legs up under herself, Taylor rolled her eyes. "For such a grounded man, you get delightful tunnel vision. Explore more carts. Live a little."

"I live plenty," he said. "I'm literally having lunch outdoors."

"You eat like you think appetites are liabilities," she said with a grin.

"And you eat like someone who's been freed."

Taylor blinked at him, surprised. "I feel it," she said after a moment. "It's been a long time, but I'm not walking on eggshells or trying to prove I deserve the space I take up."

Clinton's gaze lingered on her longer than it should have. He saw the smudge of eyeliner from too little sleep, the gentle slope of her shoulder bared where the jacket had slouched, the way she smiled with the corner of her mouth when tasting something she liked. "I like seeing you like this," he said quietly.

Her eyebrows lifted, teasing. "With sauce on my hand and lettuce in my lap?"

"With color in your cheeks," he said without flinching.

They ignored the electricity between them.

Then she flicked a drop of sauce from her sketchpad and said, "Well, lucky you. I'm available for public meals and artistic calamities most afternoons."

He chuckled once, low and warm. "I'll note that in the case file."

They ate in companionable quiet for a while, watching as a dog in a blue vest chased a flock of doves.

Taylor leaned back against the bench, sighing. "You know what's strange?"

Clinton glanced over, his expression relaxed. "Aside from us pretending this isn't a date?"

She snorted. "This isn't a date."

He didn't look away. "But if it was?"

She hesitated for half a heartbeat. Then shrugged. "If it were…you'd be doing alright."

Clinton smiled, and this time, it was full and unguarded.

"You're not too bad at this yourself."

Taylor raised her drink in a mock toast. "To excellent food and complicated definitions."

Clinton clinked his iced tea against hers with a quiet laugh. "And to taking up space without apology."

He turned toward her.

"I feel more like myself here than I ever did in L.A., and I thought L.A. was the dream."

"Maybe it was the beginning," he offered.

She glanced at him, thoughtful. "And you?"

He blinked. "What about me?"

"Is this just a job?"

He didn't answer.

"Or is it our beginning?" she asked, softer.

Clinton leaned back, the rustle of leaves blending with her breath.

"I don't know," he said, after a long beat. "This...feels like a motion set in action, and I'm still gathering the facts."

She nodded and took another bite of her pita.

He was grateful at that moment for her silence.

Chapter Twelve

Taylor

She leaned back and looked out the window of Clinton's Mercedes. The black polished leather felt cool beneath her slacks. They'd spent the better part of the day together. Outside, the sky deepened into the rich violet that signaled nightfall as headlights flickered past in silent pairs.

Taylor didn't speak. Neither did he.

Instead, their glances met and held for a beat too long, then slipped away again, drawn out and deliberately ignored. He tapped the steering wheel once, a rhythm she almost echoed with her foot.

Politeness or hesitation kept them quiet. Something had shifted, and neither of them moved to stop it.

Bailey's brownstone came into view just as Taylor took a deep breath to speak.

"You didn't have to escort me home like a visiting dignitary," she murmured finally.

When the car eased to a stop, Taylor didn't move to open

the door.

Clinton turned toward her, lips curving slightly. "You don't want to ruin your outfit in the subway."

"I rode the subway to come see you," she pointed out.

"I still stand by my decision."

Taylor studied him for a long time. The city's flickering neon caught the shadowed angles of his jaw, the weary grace in his posture. In a rare display of relaxation, he loosened his tie, revealing an exclusive vulnerability displayed only when a formal man becomes undone.

Deep in her chest, a wire snapped. "Come up," she said.

Clinton didn't flinch, but something shifted behind his eyes. "Are you sure?"

"We've had dinner, street pretzels, and a philosophical debate about morals and abstract expressionists," she replied, voice low and steady. "I'm very sure."

He hesitated just long enough for her breath to falter, but then he nodded once. "I'll park."

They didn't speak in the elevator.

By the time the loft door shut behind them, the air had changed, becoming thicker somehow, not urgent but inevitable.

Taylor dropped her keys into the bowl beside the door, then turned. Clinton stood just inside, uncharacteristically still, like he was weighing every line. He studied her sharp collarbone, the mess of her braid, the next impossibly important thing to say.

"You don't have to stay," she said, with an unsure flicker of grace.

He stepped forward instead.

The kiss wasn't hesitant.

Taylor gripped his coat lapel and rose on the balls of her feet, meeting his mouth with a fierceness made of simmered-down tension and weeks-long curiosity.

Clinton groaned against her, one hand curling around her waist, the other skimming up to rest gently at the base of her neck.

His mouth was deliberately calculated and focused, tracing the edges of her lips with an intention usually reserved for depositions and closing arguments. Still, there was something unguarded beneath it—heat, yes, but also the relief of finally naming what had been building. When she pressed closer, he adjusted to her, his palm sliding to her jaw and down the elegant line of her neck as if he were memorizing her in sections.

She matched him breath for breath, kiss for kiss—until she wasn't matching at all, but leading. Her fingers slipped up, tugging playfully at his loosened tie, and his quiet laugh landed against her mouth as he let her set the pace.

They found their way to the couch without looking, navigating half by instinct, half by the gravitational pull that had been dragging them toward this moment for weeks.

Taylor didn't fumble or glance away. She kept her eyes on his, daring him not to look away. Clinton didn't.

His hands slid along her sides, slow and steady. He didn't push. He learned. Fingertips tracing the outline of her waist, pausing when her breath caught, mapping the places that made her lean closer.

She tilted her head, testing. He didn't rush. He dropped his mouth to the line of her collarbone and kissed her there—slow, open, utterly focused.

It was enough to make her pull back and smile, breath skimming his cheek as she stood and crooked a finger for him to follow.

"This isn't a negotiation," she said, voice just a little wrecked, just a little warmed. "If you want something, take it."

The corner of his mouth tilted, but something in his gaze sharpened, losing the last of its caution. "I'm not in the business of half-measures."

"Good," she whispered, catching his loosened tie and tugging him closer by inches.

He caught her wrist. It wasn't to stop her, but to feel it, like the motion mattered. Like the permission had weight. Then he let go, and she didn't hesitate.

Their kiss deepened. It was no longer playful but laced with everything they hadn't said, hadn't dared to. Each breath, each soft pull, unfastened something tightly held.

They moved together without rushing, the space between steps collapsing as if the distance had never really existed. Her hands skimmed the crisp line of his shirt, smoothing once, anchoring herself. He shrugged out of his jacket, letting it slide over the arm of the couch without taking his mouth from hers, and she smiled against his lips like she'd won a dare.

Clinton lifted a stray curl from her cheek as if loosening a ribbon on a love letter. The soft lamplight caught the curve of her collarbone, and he stared. Grit. Grace. In every way, she stood tall even when she wanted to fold.

Every small barrier they set aside said something louder than any argument they'd had: I'm not hiding. Not from you.

They drifted, laughter catching on the threshold of the hallway when her heel bumped the baseboard and his tie landed on a chair like it had surrendered. He paused at the edge of the bedroom doorway to kiss her wrist, soft and slow, mouth brushing the delicate line where her pulse sped up. She held her breath.

Her gaze met his with something almost wild beneath it that was wonder, heat, and a feeling she didn't dare name.

He held it. Didn't look away.

"You test every limit," he murmured, like it was a truth she didn't need to defend, and maybe never had.

Her brow arched slowly. "That was a compliment?"

"Yes," he said, voice low, as he eased her back a step like she was something extraordinary. "It was."

Then he kissed her again, and gave her no more room to wonder.

She didn't retreat.

He wasn't rushing, but he was changing tactics. Less measured, more honest.

Hands slid to her hips. Lips found the sensitive curve behind her ear. His voice, quiet and steady, brushed the shell of it.

"Limit-testing doesn't scare me, Taylor. Rushing things, though? That's where I draw the line."

She swallowed hard, eyes on him now like he was the equation she suddenly couldn't solve.

He kissed her once more and let his forehead rest against hers. "We stop the second you say so."

Her hand found his, fingers interlacing. "I know."

His question lived in the pause.

She answered with a whisper that tasted like relief. "Yes. I want this. I want you here."

"Then I'm here," he said.

Consent wasn't a negotiation. It was a gift. He treated it like one. The moment deepened, and so did the way he touched her. His thumb sweeping once over the back of her hand, a quiet anchor, and his other palm warm at her waist, steadying.

They didn't need to say more. The city hummed beyond the windows, and the rest of the world fell away.

Time thinned.

They kissed until thoughts loosened and laughter threaded in, until she felt the precise point his control softened into joy. He tugged the throw from the end of the bed and wrapped it around them both, pulling her in until her forehead fit beneath his chin and their breaths matched.

There was a stretch of quiet then, thin as silk and just as strong. The kind that only happens when two people choose to be exactly where they are.

The rest of the night blurred into lamplight and whisper-soft conversation, into the sound of rain she only noticed because he did, into the warmth of his hand at the small of her back as they curled closer beneath the throw.

And then, gradually, the room dimmed to nothing but the slow, steady rhythm of shared breath.

Afterward, minutes or hours later, they lay tangled in the hush, the city a low pulse beyond the glass. Clinton's arm was beneath her, her fingers looping gently through his.

Taylor was the first to speak. "That wasn't a mistake."

"No," he murmured, brushing her hair from her cheek. "It wasn't."

She leaned into the weight of his shoulder but didn't let go of the space between them. Not yet.

They wouldn't name what this was. For now, it was shared breath, unspoken questions, and the impossibly steady beat of his heart under her ear.

Chapter Thirteen

Taylor

The kettle clicked off, and the apartment settled into a quiet she could feel in her bones. Taylor stood at the kitchen counter in thick socks and a sweater, palms wrapped around the first mug she'd touched. It was one that Candy had given Bailey last Christmas. A vintage ceramic with a gold script that read, *"Beware the Resting Whisk Face."* Ridiculous, but entertaining.

In the other room, Clinton was still sleeping.

She stirred honey into her coffee slowly, like the time and effort might guide her towards what she should do next. It didn't. The spoon clinked against ceramic, rhythmic and a little too loud.

Last night hovered at the edge of everything. How something easy had finally stopped pretending to be "just strategy." She'd wanted to sleep. Instead, her brain had hosted a round-table: logistics, feelings, and a running commentary about how she was absolutely not going to spiral.

She set the mug down and started making lists to keep

her hands busy. Fittings this week. Thread delivery. Call June about the window display. Email Clinton the updated sketch scans. She added aspirin and a glass of water to the counter because kindness didn't cost anything and also because his tie was draped over the back of a chair like a flag from a country she didn't know how to visit without a passport.

Her stomach did a traitorous little flip. She took a breath and flattened a stray Post-it with her palm.

What did this mean for them?

She didn't want to be someone's case, no matter how carefully he handled it. She also didn't want to pretend nothing had shifted. He'd looked at her last night like she was a choice, not a complication. That felt...rare.

Taylor opened her notes app, typed three lines, deleted, then grabbed a pen and wrote them by hand on the back of a bakery receipt instead:

— *I like you.*

— *I need clear lines.*

— *Let's go slow and tell the truth, even when it's awkward.*

She stuck the receipt to the fridge with a magnet shaped like a lemon. It looked ridiculous. It helped anyway.

She rinsed a handful of raspberries and arranged them in a bowl. Then she wiped the counter, straightened the salt and pepper, and pretended she hadn't just lined up his coffee next to the aspirin like she'd done it a thousand times before.

In the living room, one floorboard creaked and then went quiet. *He's not up yet.*

Good. She needed a few more minutes with her thoughts.

Taylor sat at the small table by the window, angled her

sketchbook into the light, and let her pencil move. Not gowns. Small things. A lapel that actually fit his shoulders. The clean line of a sleeve that said steady without saying stiff. She wrote the word *ask* beside a seam and underlined it twice.

Ask him what he wants.

Ask for what you need.

In the other room, the city noise thinned and returned like the tide. She took a sip of coffee and let hope and caution stand side by side without picking a winner. She could keep her work intact and still make room for a man who brought charm and hard truths, who had said she wasn't alone and made it feel like a promise instead of a platitude.

She wasn't going to hand anyone her voice again. Not Delacroix. Not fear. Not love, either. If this thing with Clinton had a real chance, it would have to fit the life she was building—not swallow it.

Taylor set out a second mug and a spoon, then sat back down and drew a steady line right through the middle of the page. Boundaries, she told herself, and let it be good.

By the time Clinton appeared, sleepy and low-voiced, Taylor stood by the stove, chewing a thumbnail while the espresso machine hissed.

"You're awake," she said around her finger, then dropped her hand.

"I heard you talking to yourself."

"Oh." She tried to sound unfazed. "Too much time alone lately, I guess."

He stepped behind her, silent, and wrapped one arm low around her waist, burying his unshaven face into her shoulder.

She exhaled, staying still.

When he pulled back, it was only enough to read her expression.

She looked at him over her shoulder. "So."

"So," he echoed, a small smile tugging at his mouth.

"Do you normally have morning-after bagels with your clients?"

He tilted his head, studying her. "You already know the answer. I've never stayed over with a client. Also, your left earring was my sock."

Taylor snorted, then sobered. "Are we okay?"

"Yes," he said without hesitation.

"But?"

He cupped her cheek. "Only if you want there to be a 'but.'"

Her heart tripped in that dangerous, meaningful way.

"I know we said simple," she said, watching his face.

"We didn't *say* anything, technically," he said. "But this doesn't feel like nothing, Taylor. Whatever this becomes, it won't distract me from helping you win."

Warmth pressed through her like a second heartbeat. She'd always known Clinton was grounded, Bailey had warned her, but now she knew what it felt like when he turned all that careful attention on her.

He kissed her temple, then stepped back.

"What do we do now?" she asked, her chin resting on his shoulder.

"Breakfast," he murmured.

"As in...French toast and emotional carbs? Or something

eggy to fortify us?"

"Somewhere in between," he said. "But definitely carbs."

"Greasy spoon or something with edible flowers and microgreens?"

He gave her a dry but affectionate look. "You'd have to present a compelling closing argument to get me to Waffle House, but I do have a spot."

"I mean…there's an awful lot I'd do for a waffle."

He smirked and kissed her shoulder. "Come on. I'll show you."

Clinton tucked his tie into his coat and gave her a crooked smile at the door.

"Thanks for giving back my shirt. Bailey would never let me live it down if her neighbors reported my walk of shame."

She arched a brow as she was putting on her earrings. "You think she *doesn't* already know? Edna in 312 is a one-woman surveillance team."

Outside, the air was crisp. Clinton pulled her close as they walked the half block to where he'd parked the night before. He opened the sleek car door for her with an easy smile.

Taylor blinked at the polished chrome. "Isn't this a nightmare in the city?"

He shrugged, more charming than sheepish. "Bit of a luxury, but I don't like waiting…or public transit."

"A little spoiled?"

"Maybe," he grinned. "But nice, right?"

She nodded, ignoring the flutter in her stomach. It wasn't just the car. It was in how easily he brushed off his privilege while taking care of himself, and everyone else, with the same precision.

The seats warmed instantly. She curled into the corner and watched the Upper West Side blur past. Clinton didn't reach for her hand or fill the silence. He just *was*—steady as a metronome.

When they pulled up to a tall brick building across from the park, a valet stepped forward.

"Good morning, Mr. Conners."

"Hi, Chet. I'm taking my friend to breakfast. We'll be a while."

"Yes, sir."

As Taylor stepped from the car, she took in the Art Deco sprawl of the building. "You live here?"

"I do."

She raised an eyebrow.

"Maybe I'll show you later...if we have time." His voice was smooth and warm. "I promised real food first."

She grinned. Didn't argue.

Two blocks later, they reached a narrow brick storefront with fogged windows and the smell of espresso in the air.

Taylor paused to read the hand-painted sign above: *Harrington's.* Inside, light and laughter spilled through the foggy glass.

Before Clinton could open the door, she touched his arm. "Are you capable of ordering pancakes without writing a brief about it?"

His mouth twitched. "Only if you promise not to critique

the syrup like it's a design metaphor."

"No promises. I'm an artist."

"You're impossible."

"You're predictable."

He opened the door and gestured grandly. "After you."

He led her to a booth by the window. A server smiled warmly. "Clinton! And with company."

Taylor pretended not to read too much into that.

"The special looks amazing," she said, scanning the menu. "Lemon ricotta crêpes and thick-cut bacon."

"My reputation is safe," Clinton replied. "But I might need to cross-examine *you* if you pick lemon over buttermilk."

"You believe classics shouldn't be touched?"

"You think citrus elevates everything?"

She grinned. "I like a little adventure."

"It's working for you."

They held each other's gaze over their coffee mugs, then Clinton said, "We can split one of each."

"Truce, but if I hate it, you're buying me a chocolate croissant."

Chapter Fourteen

Taylor

They lingered long after breakfast, tucked into the corner booth, hands always drifting. Neither was ready to say goodbye.

She nearly choked on orange juice when he told her how Bailey's parents had once hired him to clear her name after a sorority party mishap. He laughed when she admitted she had once sewn a jumpsuit backwards while distracted by *Project Runway.*

Afterward, they strolled through the park, fingers intertwined.

"I used to read here during law school," Clinton said, nodding toward a bench.

"Let me guess, you wore a tie."

"I thought it showed respect for the process."

She blinked. "That might be the most Clinton sentence I've ever heard."

They wandered through SoHo bookstores. She thumbed through fashion volumes, and he studied the antique law tomes.

"Ten bucks says you're about to find something with Latin in the footnotes," Taylor murmured, tilting her head to read the cracked spines lined up on a shelf labeled Justice & Philosophy.

Clinton gave her a sidelong look. "And you're about to spend forty-five minutes flipping through vibey editorials pretending to hate minimalism."

"That's not a denial." She grinned, plucking a hardbound volume called *Draping: Then, Now, and Always* from the display.

They meandered deeper into the narrow, labyrinthine bookstore. Taylor paused somewhere between *Mid-Century Textiles* and *Forgotten Designers of 80s Paris*. He stopped behind her as she waited at a low set of wire racks.

"Oh!" she lit up suddenly, pulling a faded French pattern book from 1973. Its cover was a dull blue with soft gold lettering, corners worn smooth.

"For when you admit linen deserves structure," she said sweetly, handing it to him like an offering.

Clinton raised a brow. "Are we still talking about fabric or your attempt to dress me in something with zero stretch?"

She shrugged. "You'll wear anything if you think it'll win the room."

"I have range."

"You have five gray suits and a rotation of smug silk ties."

He offered a mock-affronted gasp. "You forgot the navy one."

"Same smug blueprint. Different lighting."

He flipped through the old book with casual precision. "This is actually...well-argued." His tone shifted. "Look at how they reinforce the shoulder seam here. It's almost architectural."

Taylor blinked, impressed. "You know what a shoulder seam is?"

"I am dating a fashion designer."

"We're not—," she started, then caught herself. Her cheeks flushed slightly.

He looked over the book and said mildly, "Please continue."

Taylor plucked the book from his hands. "You're officially banned from technical terms unless you're actively sewing me something."

"I did iron a shirt once last year," he said. "That has to count, right?"

She snorted, then led them toward the bookstore café tucked near the back under dim lighting, with mismatched furniture, and a chalkboard sign that read: *Yes, you should get two.*

He stepped up to the counter as she perused the pastry case.

"I'll have an Americano," he said to the barista. "No milk."

"And, thank you," Taylor said, appearing at his elbow. She looked over her shoulder at the chalkboard and back again with a thoughtful nod. "And I'll have the lemon shortbread and an oat milk latte. Extra oat."

"Extra oat?" Clinton asked, amused.

"A girl's gotta watch her figure."

He leaned closer, brushing her shoulder. "I don't mind a little something to hold onto."

"Hold...or hang onto for a while."

"Which one are you leaning towards?"

"The jury's still out," she murmured.

They found a sun-dappled two-top by the window,

half-claimed by an orphaned field guide to Roman tombstones, and settled in. She tucked one leg under her. He eased out of his suit coat and rolled his sleeves slowly, the motion somehow too precise to be completely innocent.

She noticed.

"Do you always undress like that? In the middle of literary spaces?" she asked.

Clinton lifted one brow and took a sip of his coffee. "Would you prefer I did it faster?"

Taylor laughed, then crumbled a corner of her shortbread and popped it into her mouth. "I think you're trying to seduce me with professionalism."

"That obvious?"

"You're posture screams boardroom dom."

"I'll choose to take that as a compliment."

She glanced away, out the window, then leaned in conspiratorially. "I haven't felt like this in a while."

He didn't ask what she meant. He didn't need to.

He just brushed a fingertip gently over the corner of her pinky where it rested on the edge of the table.

"I like watching you like this," he said, voice low enough to hide the meaning from anyone but her.

Taylor stilled. Met his gaze.

Without breaking it, she nudged her shortbread toward him.

"Then stay right here," she said. "Eat my cookie. Judge my linen, but maybe...keep flirting like that."

He didn't smile.

He looked impressed.

And he took a bite of the cookie before asking, "Who's in charge here?"

Later, they wandered toward a food cart on the edge of Bryant Park, the air crisp with early evening promise. Lights were beginning to flicker on in the trees overhead, and the scent of roasted almonds and sugar drifted through the breeze.

Taylor leaned on tiptoes to read the menu, adjusting her sunglasses unnecessarily even though the sun was nearly gone. "Okay, but why is pistachio the perfect ice cream flavor for emotionally reserved men who secretly journal?" She asked, eyeing him sidelong.

Clinton gave a slow blink. "Who said I journal?"

She tilted her head. "I feel like you spreadsheet your feelings."

He handed a ten to the vendor. "One pistachio cone, please, and a small cup of whatever has chunks and chaos. Surprise us."

The vendor, an older man with a Mets hat and a sly grin, nodded as he spun toward the freezer. "You two a couple?"

Taylor hesitated. Clinton didn't.

"We'll plead the fifth," he said, reaching for the cone. He offered the extra cup to Taylor. It was loaded with swirls of caramel, chocolate bits, and a unique flavor derived from marshmallow fluff.

"Oh, I see," she said, inspecting her ice cream. "So, I get chaos in a cup, and you get traditional nuttiness."

He licked his cone, smug. "Balance."

"Sounds like code for 'I'm prepared to send you home with a goody bag and a goodbye, but I will remember your coffee order forever.'"

"I already do," he said.

Taylor stopped mid-bite, blinking. Then smiled. Small. Caught.

They found a bench tucked beneath a maple tree dusted with fading leaves. The noises of the city swirled around them—cabs, jazz from a passing street musician, silverware clinking from a nearby patio—but here, they sat close together in their own quiet orbit.

Taylor scooped a spoonful of her melting swirl and extended it toward him. "Try mine."

Clinton hesitated. "I don't trust things with that many ingredients."

"Says the man who eats pistachios like he's in an old noir film watching his past walk away in heels."

"Fine," he said, and leaned in. His lips brushed the spoon just slightly.

Taylor didn't move.

Their eyes locked.

Then she rolled her eyes, breaking the tension. "And?"

"It tastes like falling in love on a sugar high."

"Exactly," she said, triumphant. "It's brilliant."

They traded bites for a while, the ice cream steadily dripping down the paper cup, their shoulders tucked closer with every passing minute.

Clinton nudged her knee with his. "You know," he said, voice quieter now, "we could just call this a date."

Taylor licked her spoon, thoughtful. "Might ruin the vibe. This has the energy of those rom-coms where two overachievers fall in love by accident."

"One of them always gets ice cream on their shirt," he said.

"And the other makes fun of them but secretly finds it devastatingly charming."

He looked down.

There was a dab of pistachio on his tie.

Taylor's laughter was pure and genuine, echoing against the quiet hush of the trees overhead. She reached forward and dabbed it gently with her napkin.

Clinton didn't move.

She was still smiling when she looked up and found him already watching her.

The teasing fell away, not awkwardly, but like clothes gently shed after a long day. His gaze softened, and hers did too. For a moment, all that mattered was the warmth between them, barely bridged by melting ice cream and the tension of everything unsaid but understood.

She looked down at the last bite of swirl and handed it to him again.

Clinton took it without hesitation this time.

"I like this," she said. "The quiet. The...accidental parts."

He leaned closer. "Then let's keep getting ice cream. Until we figure out what else we like."

She leaned against him instead, the sleeves of their coats brushing, their shoulders aligned.

"This feels illegal," Taylor said.

"Eating dessert in daylight?"

"Having a day. Like this."

He nodded. "Then we plead guilty."

As the sun dipped low and shadows stretched, the end of the weekend hovered between them.

Taylor slipped her arm through his. "Can I ask something? No lawyer answers allowed."

"Unlikely, but go ahead."

She stopped walking. "Was this just a break from the case?"

He looked stunned. "I thought I was making it clear—" He took her hand. "I wanted today. Every minute."

"Even when I made you eat chaos?"

He gave her a wry grin. "That was my favorite part."

She didn't answer. Just reached up and kissed him.

It silenced the city.

When she pulled back, her breath lingered between them.

"That wasn't professional."

"No," he said hoarsely. "It really wasn't."

They walked the last eight blocks slowly.

At his building, Clinton looked from the doorman back to her. "I think I should call you a cab," he said, brushing her hand. "We both have work tomorrow."

"And neither of us wins when we rush things," she said, soft but sure. "Yet."

A slow smile tugged at his lips. "Yet."

Chapter Fifteen

Taylor

Clinton surprised her: *"Be ready by seven. Wear something you can walk in. Clinton."*

Taylor figured this meant a candlelit dinner with jazz inside one of Clinton's favorite buttoned-up steakhouses. Instead, she found him outside her building with two subway tickets clamped between his fingers and a paper bag from a bakery in his other hand. There wasn't a car or attentive driver in sight.

"I thought you only traveled in German engineered vehicles with climate control," Taylor teased, falling in beside him.

Clinton grinned, more relaxed than she'd ever seen him outside a coffee shop or a courtroom. "I do, almost always, but I like to bend the rules. Tonight, I wanted something different. A little anonymity, a little authentic New York. I'll trade my dignity for one evening on the R train if it means surprising you."

She arched a brow, delight warming her. "You're sure you can handle the lack of lumbar support?"

He let their shoulders brush as they walked. "Anyone can be driven," he added, voice lighter. "But you only feel that New York magic when you climb out of the subway and discover yourself in an entirely different life. I wanted to see the city change with you, not through a car window."

Five blocks, one crowded express ride, and a winding staircase later, Clinton led her up into a night on the West Side painted with the glow of theater marquees, every light promising something grand just out of reach. At the edge of the sidewalk, he glanced at his watch and then, as if it were the most natural thing in the world, reached for her hand.

"A Broadway show?" She asked, heart skipping the way it never had for runway lights.

"Almost." He steered her to a side street and stopped. "I thought about opera, but tonight called for something less ...predictable. The revival of On the Town. It's got dancers, spectacle, and a heroine who makes her own ending." His smile was boyish, almost bashful. "Plus, I once lost a bet to Bailey over whether I knew the difference between a pas de deux and a promenade. Cultural education, for both of us."

Taylor laughed, delighted and just a touch nervous. "This is perfect. I've never done Broadway on a weeknight."

The show itself was a riot of color and dizzying choreography, but in the cocoon of the velvet seats, Taylor found herself more aware of Clinton than anything happening under the footlights. He barely shifted, but sometimes she caught him watching her out of the corner of his eye when the orchestra swelled. He didn't reach for her, but when she let her leg brush his, he left it there, their knees leaning together, heartbeat to heartbeat.

At intermission, Clinton handed her the bakery bag. "Intermissions are long, and you skipped lunch to finalize your fitting schedule."

Inside were two miniature chocolate croissants. "You remembered," she said.

"I have an excellent memory. I know what you crave," he replied. "Food, fabric, a good story."

She looked at him, struck by the gentle intimacy buried in his everyday readiness. It made her want to share something true. "I always wanted to costume for the stage. Not just clothes, but whole lives. Sometimes I think I could've ended up backstage on a show just like this." Her voice went shy and wistful. "But I never pictured myself in the audience, or with the sort of man who'd sneak in bribes."

He drifted his fingers along the back of her chair. "I can see you behind the curtain, shaping stories with a pair of shears and an iron will. They'd never let you go."

She smiled and looked down. "What about you? What would you do if you weren't where you are?"

He hesitated, and for a moment his mask slipped. "I used to think I'd teach. My mother was a professor. I liked the idea of making things make sense for other people, but my father said there's safety in precedent, in rules. So, I became the man who writes instructions, instead."

"But you don't just follow the rules," she said. "You hold them up to the light and see through them."

He looked almost surprised by her insight. "You see me better than most people do."

She squeezed his hand, feeling the complicated blend of gratitude and fear in the tension of his palm. For once, she let herself simply stay in it, present and unguarded.

The second act was bright and brassy, audacious as New York itself. At the curtain call, Clinton leaned in, voice pitched for her ear alone. "Would you like to pull off a little iconoclasm with me?"

When they ducked out, the crowds poured toward Times Square, but Clinton led Taylor away, although she protested with a grin and the faint threat of missing her midnight train. "I want to show you something most tourists get wrong." With a practiced ease, he breezed them past security at Rockefeller Center, up the elevator, to the Top of the Rock.

The city splayed beneath them, impossibly vast and small at once, every skyscraper humming with its own private ambition. Clinton stood beside her, hands tucked in his pockets, his tie loosened just enough to suggest he was out of his element, in the best way.

Taylor pressed her forehead to the glass, taking it in. "I've visited New York over the years, but never been up here."

He watched her, not the skyline. "New York isn't about lists and landmarks. It's about all the people around you. It's about what's the same and who's different. There's always the chance you'll see something you've never seen before."

She turned. The romance wasn't in the view. It was in the admission. He wanted her to see the city his way. With him.

She looked out, then up, her profile cut in neon and shadow. He angled closer, letting the pause draw tight between them, then brushed a stray curl off her cheek. "You make New

York feel brand new," he said.

She laughed, breathless. "Dangerous line, Mr. Conners."

"I like a little danger," he answered. Then softer, "I like you."

She kissed him then, quick, her hands fisted in his lapels as he pulled her close, the city dissolving into pulse and promise behind her closed eyes. It left her devoid of practical thoughts, and feeling bright with possibility.

When they stepped back, Clinton's grin was loose and open, his thumb sweeping across her cheek, anchoring her. He looked like a man surprised to find himself exactly where he wanted to be.

"Just so you know, date night standards are now impossibly high," she whispered.

He nuzzled her hair, placing a gentle kiss just below her ear. "Then I'll have to keep outdoing myself."

They rode down through the city's heart in silence, fingers laced. Outside, the metropolis blazed. Inside, the space between them felt alive with everything unsaid, and all the time in the world to discover it.

Satisfied, Clinton hailed a cab. "No subways at midnight." He pressed a kiss to her wrist as she ducked inside, promising, "Call me when you're home safe."

She grinned. "Yes, sir."

As the city panned by the car window, Taylor could still taste his kiss. She felt hungry, not for touch, but for more of him, and all the ways being beside him made the city feel new.

Chapter Sixteen

Taylor

She adjusted the fall of the sleeve one last time, her fingers gliding along the fine silk of the dress she'd just finished fitting. The zipper slid up smoothly, hugging the client—a statuesque woman who'd spent most of the appointment murmuring excitedly into her phone—into a flowing gown with a high shoulder, low back, and a lining stitched with Taylor's signature rose-gold embroidery.

The woman gave a single spin, then settled one hand on her hip like she'd been waiting her whole life for this dress.

"Perfection," she declared to her mirror, and to whoever she was FaceTiming. "No, darling, it's not Chanel. It's Mystique." Then she winked at Taylor, ended the call, and turned. "I don't know who you are, but you're about to be everywhere."

Taylor smiled, calm and composed. "Thank you. It was my pleasure."

She left the Fifth Avenue apartment with her sewing kit in one hand and the garment bag slung over her shoulder. Her pulse buzzed with adrenaline. This mattered. This was how Mystique became more than a rumor.

Her phone buzzed as she stepped into the elevator.

Bailey.

Taylor answered immediately. "Hey, what's up?"

"Change of plans," Bailey said, her voice hoarse. "I'm sick, and Rosie's running a fever. Nothing is helping. She's had two popsicles, one meltdown, and I'm out of cough syrup."

"Oh no." Taylor winced. "Is she okay?"

"She'll survive. She's already barking orders for lukewarm ginger ale and back-to-back Sesame Street, but it means I can't be there."

Taylor froze. "Bailey?"

"You need someone to step in for the gala this weekend, and I won't be there for tomorrow's final fitting session."

"Oh," Taylor said, doing the math in her head. There was only one other person in New York who knew she was Mystique. "You're not suggesting—"

"I'm absolutely suggesting it." Bailey didn't even let her finish. "Clinton got a tux. He knows the event inside and out. Hell, he wrote up the vendor contracts and pledge forms. Plus, he's unreasonably tall and terrifyingly symmetrical. You'll finish the tailoring on the auction gown, he'll cover logistics for tomorrow, and, win-win, you won't have to go alone."

Taylor blinked. "I...what?"

"You heard me." Bailey's tone had that hands-on-her-hips energy. "He already needs to be there to go over paying the vendors and the SEC audit for pledge donors. You? You have one job. Show up and be fabulous. You don't need me for that."

Taylor stared at the wall. "This was your idea."

"Yes, and it's a good one. You're debuting as the elusive designer who sends stylists into spirals over organza. It's elegant. Efficient, and very on-brand dramatic."

Taylor pinched the bridge of her nose. "Bailey…"

"Look at it this way." Bailey's voice became sugary. "You get to pick his outfit, and you get to watch him squirm when little old ladies call him Clint."

"Bailey."

"What?"

"You don't think this is a little…loaded?"

Bailey paused. "Is it?"

Taylor opened her mouth. Closed it.

"You've been circling each other for weeks," Bailey said. "You expect me to believe it's just 'strategy sessions?'" Girl, there were fewer sparks at last year's Fourth of July picnic, and that ended with Rosie's goat leading twenty kids on a sparkler parade."

"It wasn't like that." Taylor paced through the loft, one hand on her temple. "We went to the museum. Talked logistics. Went to a show. It was very…professional." She left off at first.

"Museum dates now count as legal debriefs? Did the Met add a romance wing I wasn't aware of?"

"It wasn't a date."

"Hmm. So, you get flustered now just recounting business meetings? That's new."

"I'm not flustered!" Taylor's voice cracked. "I'm just…tired. It was a long day. There was walking, and fast food, and some light…browsing."

"Uh-huh. Maybe you got overwhelmed by all those oil paintings and saturated fats."

"Bailey, stop."

"I will, but only if you tell me why your voice does that thing it does when you're two seconds from blurting out something you'll regret."

Taylor froze.

Bailey pounced. "Oh my God. What happened?"

"Nothing," Taylor said, too fast, then softer, "I mean…nothing major. We're still figuring it out."

A beat.

"You don't have to tell me," said Bailey, gently. "But whatever stage you're in? I'm on your side."

"It's complicated."

"Then be nice to yourself while you figure it out."

"I will."

"Clinton is a professional. Whether you choose to let the romantic ambiance of the gala woo you, or you boss him around and take advantage of the fact that I'm paying him to be there, I will be grateful you aren't alone."

Taylor gritted her teeth. She hadn't planned on saying anything about her week with Clinton. Not about the loft. Not the couch. Not whispered compliments or the way his mouth moved when he kissed her.

They'd come together and then broken apart. Only to go on a date later like nothing had happened. He'd kissed her with New York shining below them, put her in a cab, said goodbye, and then they'd slipped back into crisp lines and clear boundaries. A smooth return to logistics and timelines, and careful texts that always ended in periods instead of emojis. She hadn't known whether she hated it or needed it.

And now?

Now, they'd be poured into formal wear, under flashbulbs and scrutiny, at Bailey's gala and her Mystique debut.

She shifted her weight. "It's not that simple."

"Are you worried it'll get messy?"

"I'm not afraid of messy. I didn't think I'd have to navigate it while carrying a ballgown and trying not to trip over garden lighting shaped like chandeliers."

Bailey chuckled. "Then take a breath. You don't have to name it. Just show up. Look stunning and remember he believes in you. That counts for something."

"Okay," she said at last. "You're right. I could do worse than walking into the party with someone smart, charming, and clearly has excellent taste."

"That's the spirit, Rousseau."

Chapter Seventeen

Taylor

Two hours later, Clinton stepped into Bailey's loft with a garment bag slung over one shoulder and a bottle of wine in his hand.

"This is not how I pictured an evening with you here," he said, handing her the wine.

Taylor took the bottle and raised a brow. "I'll promise to be gentle."

"Bailey said you had final approval on my gala wardrobe." He unzipped the bag holding his tuxedo and held it up. "This has gotten me through more events than I care to count."

"Which is exactly the problem," she muttered, reaching forward. "Look at this lapel. Too wide. This satin stripe is a decade old."

"It's timeless," he argued.

"It's tired," she countered.

Taylor smoothed the silk of the tie with a precision that made the air between them pulse. "When, exactly, did you last wear this?" she asked, brow arching.

Clinton gave a slight shrug. "Three fundraisers ago. Possibly a chamber of commerce speech. Hard to remember, they hand out cocktails and pretend they like your tie."

"Well," she murmured, lifting his lapel and pressing it flat with her palm. She pinned and tucked while taking notes. "They lied. This is tragic."

"Tragic?" he echoed, mildly offended. "I've been told I look 'commanding' in this suit."

"By whom? A mirror with low self-esteem?"

He let out a soft laugh. "Remind me again why I'm letting you dress me?"

"Because you asked for my professional opinion, and you're smart enough to know when you need an upgrade." Her fingers lingered at his collarbone a beat longer than necessary before she ran her hands down the dark fabric. "And because you like it when I boss you around."

Clinton tilted his head. "There's limited evidence of that."

"You literally showed up early, with dry cleaning and back-up cufflinks."

He grinned, hands still loosely at his sides. "I assumed you'd disapprove of the originals."

"I did. Vehemently."

He arched a brow. "And what do you suggest?"

She paused a beat, then disappeared to the garment rack in the corner. She returned with a deep navy velvet jacket, slim through the waist, with a slightly exaggerated shawl collar and silk-covered buttons that glinted in the light like sequins hidden in seriousness.

Clinton's jaw twitched. "You want me to wear couture."

"I want you to dress like you belong there." Taylor folded the jacket over her arm and gestured for him to hold out his arms. "This jacket doesn't scream luxury. It murmurs it. Respectfully."

He hesitated for only a second, then obeyed.

As she slipped the new jacket over his shoulders and smoothed the sleeves down his arms, Taylor couldn't pretend her hands weren't interested in the territory they passed. He smelled expensive. He wore a cologne that was spicy and woodsy, like pine polished with bourbon.

"You're very good at this," he said, voice low.

She didn't look up. "I slept under mannequins in fashion school. I once basted a hem with a tampon string on a train home because my thread snapped. You learn."

He laughed, a quick breath that filled the small space between them.

Her hands moved to the lapel, adjusting the fold, then pressing the shoulders, so the seams sat along his frame just right. She stepped back, then tilted her head.

"There," she said. "You were tolerable before, but now?"

"Devastating?" he offered.

"Distracting," she corrected.

He blinked. "That's not what I expected from you."

Taylor blinked too, then let her hands fall from the fibers of the jacket, brushing her fingertips against his wrist as she turned away.

"Well, get used to it," she said lightly. "Mystique doesn't do forgettable."

Clinton adjusted the cuffs as she walked over to a table littered with fabric scraps and garment chalk.

"So," she said after a beat, as she examined a swatch of midnight silk, "we're hosting a masked gala built to disguise my identity while also putting my designs on display for all his friends, clients, and press contacts." She glanced back at him. "Does that feel mad to you?"

"No. It feels brilliant and dangerous," he said, removing his cufflinks one at a time. "A perfect plan if you'd like to light a string of matches behind you while walking into the lion's den in high heels."

She grinned. "Three-inch heels. Maybe four."

He gave her a look. "And what are you wearing?"

"You'll see."

Clinton watched her fingers flutter over her sketches, quiet and efficient. "There'll be media."

"Bailey says the theme is Secrets & Signatures. Most won't know who anyone is, let alone me."

Clinton said nothing.

"You look good in velvet," she added, voice softer.

He was close enough now to notice the way the light caught the silver cuff bracelet peeking out from beneath her sleeve.

She guided him to the hallway mirror, the soft gold sconces making the room glow. She moved behind him like a general inspecting a soldier.

"Tie?" she asked.

He handed her the bowtie. "You really don't like this tux."

"I really don't like the fact that you wore this to, I'm guessing, more than half a dozen black tie galas, a few distillery award dinners, and, quite possibly, a funeral or two.”

He stood still under her hands.

Taylor stepped back and surveyed him. “Better. Still not perfect,” she added, walking a slow half circle. “But the pote ntial...it’s there.”

He let his gaze linger on her lips. “Then what’s the verdict, Your Honor?”

She gave him another once-over, crisp tux and artfully di-sheveled hair now working in perfect harmony. “You might even pass for fashionable.”

“I’ll take it,” he said, his voice low. “Coming from you, that sounds like a confession.”

Taylor leaned against the wall, studying more than the suit. “Walk toward me,” she said.

He blinked. “Excuse me?”

“I need to see how it moves. Go.”

He walked. Slowly. Eyes on her.

She swallowed. “Again.”

He did. The jacket flared just slightly at his hips, bending to his posture.

“You stand straighter than most men,” she said quietly, stepping toward him again.

She tugged at the sleeve length. Pressed the side seams flat. Her hands explored the fit across his chest.

“You’re all edges and sharp lines. This jacket wants to fight that. Let me fix it.”

His voice was low. “You’re dangerously close to flirting with fabric metaphors.”

“Stop me.”

He didn't.

The mirror caught them both. He in the suit adjusted it to frame the broad shape of his shoulders and his flat waist, while she, behind him, wore leggings and a charcoal gray sweater with threads clinging to the sleeves. In the reflection, the contrast didn't clash. It clicked.

Taylor met his eyes in the mirror.

"You wear the suit like you wear everything else," she murmured, smoothing the shoulder seam. "Casually confident. I think you'd go to the gala in gray sweatpants if you could."

"I hear they're very flattering," he said, barely audible.

"For the right...body type," she corrected.

"How's my body?"

"Fishing for compliments?"

"No, just...getting your professional opinion."

Her hand paused on his shoulder. Then, maybe without meaning to, slid down past the lapel and over his chest. Slowly. Thoroughly.

"I wasn't sure you cared about my opinion of your body."

His breath hitched.

"Why would you say that?"

Taylor's eyes dropped. "I couldn't tell if you were pulling back. Maybe you regret..."

"Don't. No."

He turned slightly, and the switch flipped.

The moment their mouths met, the question that had hovered between them all week vanished. Hunger took its place—cleaner now, unfiltered. His kiss wasn't tentative. It was decisive, without hesitation.

Taylor grinned against it, tugged at his lapel until the jacket slipped free.

She let it fall to the floor.

"I could be wrong, but wrinkles aren't likely to make the suit look any more appealing," he murmured as she backed toward the couch.

"I'll steam it later," she replied, already loosening his tie. "Or not."

He laughed low, genuine, already a little undone.

When her calf hit the edge of the couch, she let herself sit, tugging him with her. His weight followed slowly, caging her in but not consuming her. They found their rhythm quickly—restraint giving way to something easy.

Taylor arched, fingers between shirt buttons, dragging him closer with each breath.

They hadn't touched for six days—on purpose. Strategy. Boundaries. All good ideas. None helpful now.

Her palm slid beneath the hem of his shirt, just enough to feel his warmth.

He cursed softly against her mouth.

She didn't answer, just leaned up, met his mouth again, unbothered by pleats or propriety.

This wasn't their first time.

But it was the first time they didn't hold back their hearts.

By the time his hands skimmed beneath her sweater, it wasn't with curiosity. It was certainty. His fingers traced a map of her—ribs, spine, the steady line of her shoulder blades.

He drew her in with a firm grip at her hips, kissed her hard and deep until her breath stuttered, then eased them both down onto the cushions. She let out a surprised, breathy laugh against his lips, her fingers tangling in the front of his shirt.

They sank onto the couch together, laughter bumping into cushions and a throw pillow skittering to the floor like it had been waiting for company. Her hands slipped beneath his jacket to ease it from his shoulders, fingertips tracing the line of his sleeve as she asked, "How many times have you analyzed the structural integrity of this couch?"

"Just enough to know it won't break beneath us," he said, his grin brushing her temple as he bent close, voice warm at her ear.

She laughed and tucked her legs under herself, knees knocking softly against his.

He tipped his forehead to hers, then pressed a quiet kiss to her cheek, the corner of her mouth, her brow.

Their kiss deepened, not hurried, not showy. He wasn't tentative now. Confident without pushing, he studied the places she relaxed—the way her shoulders eased, the way her jaw unclenched. One hand settled at her waist, the other open over her midriff, steadying the rise and fall of her breath.

Taylor leaned into his touch, her breath catching. Her hands framed his face, and her voice dropped to a whisper. "Clinton..."

He paused, eyes searching hers.

"You're sure?" he asked, one brow tilting in a way that was all formality with a thread of genuine vulnerability woven through it.

"I'm not just sure," she whispered, smile flickering. "But, I'd like you to stop overthinking."

That did it.

He huffed a soft, helpless laugh against her hair and shifted only enough to tuck her closer, not to press but to anchor, a low breath catching between them.

On the table, the soft measuring tape he'd used earlier lay coiled like a ribbon. He reached for it, then stopped—changed his mind—and instead lifted her wrist and pressed a kiss where a bracelet might rest.

"Okay?" he murmured. "If I keep kissing you like this?"

She nodded.

"Words, please," he said against her mouth, gentle. "Only if you want it."

"Yes," she said, and the smile that followed belonged only to him.

He laced their fingers, set her hand over his heart, and the world narrowed to the simple things: the warm press of palms, a shared breath, the soft slide of wool and silk, the hush that comes when two people stop pretending they aren't already all in.

The city hummed outside the windows. Somewhere, a horn blared. In here, the light dimmed, laughter threaded through kisses, and their conversation turned quiet and close—snippets of story, small confessions, and the sort of comfortable silence that feels like a promise—until the room itself seemed to exhale.

Later, under the throw, with the city's glow flickering across the ceiling, they lay tucked together on the couch. His tie hung loose from the armrest, and her sweater was hitched at one shoulder. Clinton shifted to kiss her temple.

Then he whispered, "I need to prepare you."

"For what?" Taylor turned slightly in his arms, half-shielded by the blanket. "I'm not ready for another round of reality just yet."

"The gala," he said. "Delacroix's PR team will be there. I already confirmed it through a contact this afternoon. They're sniffing for stories. If they start digging into Mystique, we have to be ready."

The moment snapped like a blown thread.

Taylor pulled the blanket higher. "Of course they'll dig. That's what they do."

He brushed her hair gently back from her forehead. "This doesn't change anything. I'm still with you."

But something in her had closed—just a little.

She didn't doubt him. She was doubting how long she could keep both of her worlds stitched together before the seams started pulling. But she didn't say it.

Instead, she pressed a kiss to his collarbone and whispered, "I know."

But even as Clinton pulled her closer, she was already listening for the sound of unraveling.

At the gala, under chandeliers and champagne and curated chaos, she wouldn't get to hide behind strategy and stitching.

They would all be watching.

Chapter Eighteen

Taylor

Ribbons of silver light streaked through the glass-domed ceiling of the ballroom, the chandeliers above glittering like constellations in full bloom. Outside, the gala's signature "bronze carpet" was a deep golden shade reminiscent of barrel-aged whiskey that stretched from the valet line to the grand front arch, flanked by branded florals and columned lanterns glowing blush and pearl.

It was a circus of refinement. Only New York's elite could orchestrate such a spectacle with couture gowns, delicately manufactured scandals, and luxury masks priced higher than most mortgages.

But tonight, none of it—not the champagne towers, nor the rose-scented dry ice, not even the stiletto-lined staircase—could compete with the gowns.

Mystique's gowns.

Her clients did not disappoint. She had fitted and styled more than half a dozen women there, and they'd done what they do best. Each glided through the press line like living artwork. Their necks glittered with diamonds, their masks were custom-designed by Tiffany's, and their hair was sculpted to architectural precision.

That alone was impressive, but her dresses stole the show. They shimmered over curves like poured light. Hemlines whispered across the marble in layers of dusk-toned silk and featherweight tulle, each stitch a secret, each movement a question.

Who was behind these gowns?

The mystery had caught fire. Every murmur, every second glance, every collective pause in conversation poured gasoline on the blaze.

Taylor stood tucked just inside the archway, half-concealed in the shadows behind the gala's grand entrance corridor. Her own gown was a deep aubergine creation with precision-cut seaming and a cathedral-split train. It hugged her curves. The mask Bailey had sent her shimmered in intricate metallic beadwork, veiling the bones of her face but leaving her eyes wide and exposed.

"Easy," Clinton murmured beside her.

His tuxedo had been altered precisely to her specifications, with a leaner silhouette cut than he was used to. Sleek lapels, better lines. He looked devastatingly composed; his ivory mask was a minimalist contrast that made his eyes sharper, colder.

Taylor didn't answer right away. Her hands clenched the gilded clutch at her side.

"They're loving it," he said, tilting toward the crowd just beyond the entrance arch. His voice was casual, but she recognized the gleam in his eyes. He'd been tracking engagement metrics since the bronze carpet reveal began forty-five minutes ago. "#MaskedInMystique is trending in Paris. LA. Dubai."

"And here?" she asked.

He met her gaze. "Here, you've already won."

She exhaled.

Together, they stepped forward. Clinton kept half a pace behind, a quiet act of deference as an usher gestured them into the ballroom.

Inside, masked guests glittered like confetti falling under soft purple lights. Tiers of calligraphed seating cards flanked the reception table, and across the room, baubles sparkled from every hemline.

One woman, trussed into a sapphire column gown, nearly lost her footing and was caught by a man who murmured, "Perhaps you should have requested a Mystique. Those are clearly made for impact, and for the woman wearing them."

Toward the back, an elevated display gleamed with LED panels scrolling real-time social media reactions from the bronze carpet outside. Taylor watched her designs flash across the screen; each post tagged with increasingly obsessive captions: *"Mystique isn't a name. It's a #revolution." and "I'd trade my ex-husband's alimony for one of my own."*

Clinton leaned in. "Your anonymity is the most photographed thing in the room."

That made her laugh. "To exposure," she said, accepting a flute of champagne from a passing server.

"To containment," he replied, clinking his glass against hers.

The ballroom glowed. Light bounced off gilded mirrors

and shimmered across the champagne flutes. Taylor sipped slowly from her glass, the beadwork on her gloves catching the glow of chandeliers overhead. All around her, elegance bloomed in layers. Metallic silks were brushing marble floors, tuxedoed servers gliding through the crowd with flutes of something chilled and golden, and a string quartet tucked beneath an arch of dripping wisteria, playing a lilting version of a late-aughts pop song that no one admitted they recognized.

"Mystique gowns at tables three, six, nine...and seventeen," Clinton murmured, the satisfaction unmistakable.

She nodded, swallowing the grin threatening to escape. "It's surreal."

Taylor had been designing dresses and taking fitting appointments for weeks, but the seamstresses had finished the dresses. She'd touched each fabric art piece, yet she hadn't seen the final dresses on all the women. She'd flooded New York society with her work, but only a few people had actually stood in a room with her. Even fewer knew she was the designer herself, not an assistant taking measurements, and all had signed NDAs agreeing to keep what they learned confidential. They probably weren't intimidated by the thought of Clinton enforcing their legal obligation, but more likely motivated by a desire to keep her secret, fearing she'd never design for them again.

But she could feel the buzz in the room, like static against her skin. Her secret was safe, for now, but her designs had stepped into the light.

One by one, the gowns had floated in on stylists, CEOs, and a certain openly catty duchess with sharp cheekbones and a sharper tongue swept past and smirked, whispering, "You'll want to keep your eye on Mystique."

Bailey's planning was faultless. A cascade of silver tones draped the central tables, flickering over floating LED candles in black-water bowls. Gold-foiled place cards framed each setting, along with art pieces made by local students. Each element was a soft reminder of the evening's mission to support arts equity in underfunded schools.

But it was the auction that transformed admiration into obsession.

Taylor stood just beside a marble riser near the front as Clinton clasped his hands behind his back and watched the frenzy unfold.

The gown up for auction, a Mystique original created in secrecy, rested on a backlit podium. Sequins traced their spine like constellations. The neckline was high in front, scandalously low in back, whispering command and confidence with every fold.

The MC stepped up. "Ladies and gentlemen, we are honored to present a never-before-seen design, donated by fashion's most enigmatic force. A Mystique original. One of one. Never to be repeated."

The crowd surged closer. Phones lifted. A stylist in feathers hissed something to her assistant.

"Starting bid is five thousand."

An arm went up. Then another.

"Ten."

"Fifteen."

"Twenty-five," someone called before the auctioneer could finish the increment.

The numbers climbed.

"Thirty-six, from the back row."

"Forty."

"Forty-five from the woman in the peacock wrap."

Taylor's pulse jumped as the bid crossed fifty. Her face flushed, not from nerves, but sheer, unfiltered pride.

She thought about her signature embroidered inside. In this room, Mystique had become real. It was her dream stitched into each seam, built from silent years and stolen credit. Everything had been heading towards this moment.

"Sold," the announcer said finally, a gavel tapping to thunderous applause. "Mystique's custom piece will now reside in the Met's costume archive, alongside a generous donation from tonight's winner."

Taylor gasped, then laughed, gripping Clinton's elbow to stay upright.

"You just landed yourself in a museum," he murmured, pride warming his voice.

"It's insane."

"It's deserved."

And this time, she believed it.

As the string quartet began a slow waltz and slices of lavender-glazed cake were passed on gold-rimmed plates, a particular hum settled over the crowd. That unspoken charge when a room knows something monumental just happened.

Taylor allowed herself to breathe. Her shoulders eased back. The ache behind her knees lessened as she moved to her heels. Her body, so often clenched with caution, uncoiled. The praise settled gently across her skin. For just a moment, she forgot to be afraid.

She didn't see him at first. She heard him.

The crowd stilled. Cameras began clicking in rhythm. The hush rolled in like a change in weather.

Clinton's hand tightened at the small of her back.

Taylor turned.

And there he was.

Laurent Delacroix.

He wore black, always black, but tonight's tux was a regal textured velvet. His mask gleamed like polished obsidian. His smile sliced through the crowd like a blade.

And when his eyes found Taylor as Mistique, he didn't blink.

Then, he stopped. So did everyone else.

"Haven't we met before?" His voice cut through the stillness like the opening of a play.

Taylor's breath caught. The ballroom spun.

Would he recognize the woman the girl he knew had become?

Clinton shifted forward, body angled just slightly in front of hers.

"Sir," he said, calm but firm.

But Laurent kept walking.

"If I didn't know better," he said, smile gleaming, "I'd swear you look familiar, dear lady."

Flashes sparked. The rustle of guests shifting, shoes, and silk brushing against parquet floors was deafening.

"Which designer are you wearing?" a reporter called. "Are you Mystique?"

Laurent smirked. "She certainly wears it like she knows where it was born."

Taylor's tongue stuck to the roof of her mouth. Don't flinch, she thought. Don't run. She could only stand her ground because her limbs wouldn't move.

Clinton stepped fully into view. "She's wearing a commissioned piece for this gala," he said coolly. "And since this has turned personal, let me be clear."

He reached back and took Taylor's left hand in his.

"This is my fiancée. We're here for the cause, not the drama."

The word echoed.

Fiancée.

Gasps rippled.

Taylor stared at him, stunned, but Clinton didn't flinch.

"You've already been told you weren't welcome here," he said, low but sharp. "I don't believe I was unclear."

Laurent's eyes narrowed. "I bought a seat. I have as much right to be here as she does."

Clinton's voice didn't rise. "Since slander's easier than truth, let me make this easy for you. Walk away."

The cameras were doubling. Reporters covered their mics, grasping to plan new angles. Spotlights spun toward the corridor Clinton aimed them toward, and all around them, the illusion cracked.

Taylor couldn't breathe.

Clinton angled her behind his shoulder just enough to block the view.

"You're shaking," he murmured against her ear. "Come

with me. Now."

She nodded.

They hurried past half-empty champagne flutes and startled glances into a curtained hallway beyond mirrored French doors.

The sound faded once they slipped behind a pair of mirrored French doors and into a backstage hallway dimmed down to a warm steel glow.

Taylor pressed against the wall, trembling.

Clinton closed the door behind them and stood between her and everything outside.

"They'll clear it," he said quietly. "Molly will handle the press spin. Bailey's team will kill the footage. He won't find your name tonight."

"But everyone was looking," she whispered. "He saw me, and you! Why didn't you tell me he'd be here?"

"He wasn't supposed to be," Clinton said. "He tried to arrange for tickets. We declined. Politely. Apparently, that didn't work."

"The confidence! He acted like I owed him."

"You don't owe him anything," Clinton said fiercely. "He lost the only leverage he ever had. Now he'll grasp the narrative. That doesn't mean he gets to take one more thing from you."

She was shaking again. "He gets to act like I'm the fraud."

Clinton stepped closer. "You are the creator—the vision. Nothing out there was his. He didn't see a victim, Taylor. He saw a threat, and he panicked."

Tears rimmed her lashes, not from fear, but rage.

"I hate that he gets to be the one asking questions," she said, voice fragile. "That he gets to act like I'm the thief."

"He doesn't," Clinton said. He took her clenched fists in his. "You are the designer. You are the creator. Nothing out there came from him. It was all you. The only theft here is how long he's kept that truth buried."

A silence bloomed between them.

Then, Taylor whispered, "Thank you, but...my fiancé?"

"My secret...always keep them guessing." Clinton tilted his forehead to hers. "I'm right here."

Outside, the camera flashes kept popping, but inside that tucked hallway, behind velvet swaths of privilege and power, Taylor realized something terrifying and true.

The fight was now public.

Chapter Nineteen

Taylor

Beneath the buzz of fluorescent bulbs and the smell of dust and metal stairs, she looked up. Clinton hovered near the landing, watching her. Jacket unfastened, bowtie loose. Something tense still lived in the set of his shoulders.

"We can't go back just yet."

"How long will it take for security to clear the area?"

"I don't know. They're going to text me. Then we can grab your things and go. I think there's been enough excitement for tonight."

"So, we're just waiting here trying to pass the time."

Their eyes met.

She stepped forward, and he met her halfway.

Clinton reached for her face with one hand. He let his palm skim along her cheek, ending with his thumb resting beneath her jaw like a question that didn't need words. Her breath caught.

Then he kissed her: no preamble, no performance, and no

calculation.

Just heat.

It wasn't polished or polite. It was everything they hadn't said for weeks and held tight between stitched seams and strategic pacing—now unraveled at the speed of a heartbeat.

His other hand circled her waist, drawing her in gently as he deepened the kiss.

Taylor didn't flinch.

She surrendered, leaning into him as if gravity had been holding her back until this very second. The world narrowed to his mouth on hers, the sure grip of his hand at her side, the whisper of breath that passed between them like something sacred.

Her fingers curled into the front of his shirt, anchoring herself. The soft cotton bunched beneath her nails, and she dragged him closer as if anything less than complete contact would undo her.

She didn't kiss him gently. Not with so much undone inside her.

Nothing was flattering about the moment. The stairwell lighting was sharp and unfriendly, flickering against exposed pipes and scuffed cement. Her couture gown was askew, twisted slightly on her frame from the hurried retreat. One heel was half off. Hairpins had scattered hours of effort in a single pivot. Her once-perfect makeup had abandoned its post hours ago leaving streaks of mascara beneath her eyes and the remnants of lipstick softened by nerves, champagne, and grief.

But this wasn't the polished version of herself. This was Taylor raw. Taylor unraveling. The version that was out of her mind and kissing a man she shouldn't want as badly as she did because he was the only real thing left in a room full of flashbulbs and fraud.

She pulled back slightly, breath shaky against his mouth, but not retreating. "You tried to prepare me, but I wasn't ready for tonight," she whispered.

Clinton's hand moved from her waist to her jaw, thumb brushing the line where her smudged makeup ended. He didn't flinch. He didn't joke.

"You did just fine. Everyone saw you," he said. "And, despite seeing you, they have no idea what they're looking at."

She let out a wet laugh, blinking up at him through lashes kissed with mascara and salt.

Behind them, the echoes of the gala buzzed. Music pulsed faintly through the thick door, and laughter rose and fell like a wave. Here, pressed between worn concrete and the man who had just called himself her fiancé without missing a beat, was the stillness she'd been so desperately trying to find.

Clinton leaned in again and kissed her like the world could wait.

Their mouths met, not in frenzy, but in affirmation as a quiet promise written in breath and skin.

When they finally broke again, Clinton rested his forehead against hers. "You did everything right in there."

"I froze."

"You stood." He met her gaze. "You didn't run."

"Because I froze, but I guess as long as it looked convincing." Taylor nodded once, then sagged forward until his chest caught her. "I don't feel brave, just...officially exhausted."

He smiled against her temple and kissed the space beneath her ear. "You're both. That's the trick."

She felt his slow exhale anchoring her. Taylor could barely finish the thought that started in her spine. He was steady. Of course, he was steady. Now, unbelievably, he was hers.

"I didn't plan on that," she whispered, her laugh breaking around the edges.

"I think we both knew something like that would happen tonight," he murmured, thumb tracing the curve of her jaw, voice rough. "We just didn't want to admit we wanted it."

She opened her eyes.

Everything about him felt like grounding. He was the center of gravity in a room that wouldn't stop spinning.

"I'm not just fighting this because he's wrong," Taylor breathed. "I'm fighting because...I want to see how far I make it when I stop apologizing for being the one who made the thing. When I stop hiding."

His smile wasn't bright. It was something quieter. Something earned.

"And maybe," she added, curling her fingers around his lapel, "because I'm not done fighting for you either."

Something in him shifted at that.

He kissed her once more. Slower. Fiercer.

In the half-lit heat of the stairwell, Taylor felt something click into place.

They slipped out the back exit when security texted. The night air was cool against the heat on her cheeks. Clinton didn't make a production of it. He found her a bottle of water from a street vendor, handed her his jacket when the wind lifted, and walked her home through quieter streets where the city's noise softened to a hum.

"Tea or toast?" he asked in the elevator, voice low, like they might startle the moment if they spoke too loud.

"Both," she said, then, because the truth was more tender than she liked to admit, added, "And you. Just for a little while."

The magic of the gala was hours behind them now, stripped away like costume jewelry after curtain call. Even the hush of applause, if that's what tonight had been, was falling silent.

Taylor curled on her side on top of the covers, a soft robe knotted at her waist and a cup of chamomile cooling on the bedside table. Clinton sat beside her, shoes off, jacket draped over a chair, tie unknotted and forgotten. Their clothes hung in the closet.

They hadn't planned to stay together. Not officially, but they hadn't been able to walk away either. Not tonight.

He didn't ask to stay; he asked if she wanted company. She nodded and handed him a second pillow as an answer.

There'd been no second-guessing after the door latched and the quiet settled. No strategy. No spin. Just the simple rhythm of rinsing off makeup, trading glitter for comfort, and watching steam curl from two mugs on the nightstand while the city breathed beyond the windows. They talked in murmurs and smiles that didn't need words. The lights clicked off. He stretched out over the quilt beside her, not crossing a line, just finding her hand and threading their fingers like a promise that didn't need a contract.

Now the room was hushed but not empty. The city yawned outside, Manhattan light bleeding across the bedroom like a soft reminder that they weren't completely hidden, no matter how well the shadows wrapped them.

Taylor sighed, then shifted, fitting her leg more tightly under the throw. Clinton didn't wake, but his arm drew her close without thought—over the blanket, over the robe—steady, like instinct.

She didn't want to sleep. She wasn't sure what part of her refused. Perhaps it was the part that still didn't trust peace, or maybe the part that didn't know what morning would bring.

The glitter of the press still clung to her like static electricity. Mystique had walked into the gala tonight to whispered gasps, champagne toasts, the subtle tilt of Vivienne Chen's approving head, and she had survived it.

But the price of the disguise was mounting. Every step forward invited new questions. How long could secrecy be a selling point? How long before anonymity became a liability?

Clinton stirred slightly, a faint grunt escaping as he rolled toward her, bringing her with him by the hand he still held. His palm rested warm and solid on the middle of her back, fingers splayed in a quiet anchor.

Still half-asleep. Still wrapped around her like she was something worth keeping.

They hadn't talked about what came next. Not really. Just numbers and logistics about pledge percentages, payment processors, and a surprise spike in donations. Clinton had grinned and kissed her temple like they'd won something.

In the quiet, Taylor kept thinking of the girl she'd glimpsed in the mirror hours earlier. Coral lipstick. Crystals in her hair. Shoulders bare beneath the shimmer of silk. She'd looked like someone else, and maybe that was the point.

Mystique needed a mask, but Taylor Rousseau was still mending herself. Not just her work but fixing the part in herself that hadn't quite made peace with belonging. With being seen. With being loved out loud.

She hadn't told Clinton that yet. Not fully. He probably already knew.

He shifted again, his cheek brushing hers. One eye blinked open drowsily.

"You're awake," he murmured, voice thick with sleep.

She nodded. "Couldn't turn it off."

"Want me to distract you?"

A small smile touched her lips. She shook her head. "Just. ..don't let go."

In answer, he tucked her closer, his thumb moving in small circles just beneath the ridge of her shoulder blade.

"I couldn't even if I tried," he murmured, half-asleep again.

But she was wide awake, eyes fixed on the ceiling, heart calibrated to the sound of his breath slowing beside hers.

She wasn't sure what tomorrow would bring. Headlines, late-night phone calls, or flashbulbs pointed in the wrong direction. The unraveling might start soon.

But for now, beneath these covers, beneath this man, in this quiet, measured comfort, she wasn't anything other than warm and wanted.

The night thinned around them, the city a soft hush beyond the glass. She pressed a kiss to his knuckles, let her eyes drift closed, and trusted the dark to hold its curtain where they'd drawn it.

She exhaled and tried to relax, as if sleep could be a choice.

Chapter Twenty

Taylor

The exposed brick felt like possibility.

Taylor stood barefoot in the center of the open studio, her arms crossed over a slouchy gray sweater dotted with flecks of thread. Outside, the streets of Chelsea hummed. Inside, the hush was thick with promise.

The space, technically a converted storage floor above a former art supply store, was hers—all six hundred square feet of it. The floors were cement, vintage-postcard gray with specks of old paint like accidental constellations. Skylights stretched unevenly across the ceiling, dusty but luminous, casting a hazy light that shifted with the hour. It was a light you couldn't buy, and it came with age and history and imperfections tailor-made for inspiration.

The walls carried the ghost of charcoal and turpentine, a trace of the artists who'd come before. A retired drafting table sat in one corner with an uneven leg and a lifetime's worth of scars. She'd already claimed it for sketching. Exposed wiring ran the length of one wall, coaxed into copper conduit with a charming stubbornness.

The windows framed a crooked view of SoHo rooftops, where pigeons held court on chimneys that leaned like old men in conversation. Below, the sidewalks buzzed with too much speed, but up here the world moved at half-speed.

There wasn't signage yet. No staff. Just her breath fogging the glass and a to-do list as long as a ballgown hem. If she tilted her head just right, she could see it. There were spools of thread arranged in rows, muslin mockups pinned with precision, and a line of vintage dress forms along the far wall. If she let herself believe it, there would be an intern or two learning to use their hands before they tried to use their names.

She'd signed the lease that morning and emptied the last of her savings to do it.

"It'll be okay," she said aloud to the empty room. "I'm investing."

The words echoed back a little too quickly, like even the walls weren't sure they believed her. She stood taller anyway, chin lifted toward the cracked ceiling of her rented studio. If she didn't act like she believed in this, who else would?

Taylor glanced around at the open space that still smelled faintly of fresh paint and cardboard glue. The vintage dress forms she'd ordered on clearance leaned against the far wall, and a half wall of scratched wooden shelves, wiped clean and waiting, stood like sentinels. This place wasn't ready yet. Neither was she, but that had never stopped her before.

This wasn't Serenity. It wasn't the boutique with the chipped window decals and the bell that jingled five seconds too late. That little shop had been a lifeline once. It was a soft landing after LA had burned her raw. Lately, it felt like a beautiful echo. Something she'd shed but not discarded.

She loved that shop, filled with comfort and familiarity. It still ran with the help of her assistant, June, who texted every few days with order updates and mild disasters solved with ingenuity and patched seams. Taylor hadn't been there for weeks. She wasn't curating inventory anymore. She was creating it. Her name was still on the shop door, but her hands weren't behind the counter.

What had been her beginning wasn't her ending.

This studio—this space, this city—felt like the life she'd spent years designing in her daydreams. Finally, she was brave enough to live it.

Yes, it meant more distance from home. Yes, it meant risking everything. It wasn't only her savings, but her anonymity, her footing, her heart. Mystique had caught fire, and if she wanted to do more than watch it crackle from the sidelines, she had to be here. In it. Present. Unhidden.

Clients were reaching out. Stylists were name-dropping her as if she'd already secured next season's A-list designers. She knew she already had a place in fashion history, but she didn't want to be just a blip on the timeline. Clinton was drafting legal protections around her sketches like armor. Even Bailey had described Mystique as "an emerging powerhouse brand," and Bailey did not exaggerate about business. Ever.

Taylor swiped a length of silk across the table, letting it pool in her hand. It was heavy and expensive, but it shimmered with light like endless possibilities.

This wasn't about leaving Serenity behind.

It was about moving forward with eyes wide open.

She flattened her hand against the cool surface of the sewing table.

Fear lingered.

But so did every reason to keep going.

"I'm not panicking," she said again, quieter this time. "I'm investing. In me."

Her voice echoed off the blank walls like a dare.

Twenty minutes later, Clinton knocked once and stepped inside. He didn't remove his coat; instead, he kept one hand wrapped around a legal envelope and the other tapping a clipboard that looked like it had survived Y2K.

"This is where you're setting up shop?" He turned slowly, gaze sharp. "I'm guessing the charm outweighs zoning compliance?"

"It has character," she said defensively, pulling her sweater sleeves down over her hands. "And excellent light."

He turned toward the floor-to-ceiling window, brow furrowed. "And structural concerns. You can see where the wall's shifted. It's not stabilized post-renovation."

"They gave me a discount," she said quickly, lifting her chin. "And it passed inspection. Mostly."

He turned to her, one eyebrow raised. "I would've reviewed the contract. If you'd asked."

"If I asked," she echoed. "And we both know how that

would've gone."

Clinton stepped toward her, careful, like he was trying not to step on whatever line she was in the middle of drawing. "I'm here now. Do you want help, or not?"

Taylor narrowed her eyes. "Which version? The one with red-ink corrections, or the one with barely concealed judgment about how I'm risking everything on a space with peeling caulk and a ghost problem?"

He exhaled through his nose. "I'm not trying to—"

"Criticize?" she snapped. "Because you're doing a great impression."

"I'm offering you security."

"I didn't ask for security. I asked for space. I'm scared, Clinton. I'm *trying* something. Instead of asking how it feels to build from scratch again, you're lecturing me about building codes."

They stared at each other.

His jaw flexed. "It's because I care."

"For me, or about the risk?"

"With you," he said. "It's always been with you."

The silence stretched.

Taylor blinked, her anger coiling and uncoiling just beneath her ribs. "And what does that mean, exactly? Because I've been hearing legal advice from your mouth and feeling something else from your hands."

He didn't answer.

Instead, he stepped forward and held out the envelope.

She opened it warily.

She opened it slowly. Inside, tucked between lease addenda and a file labeled *Operations,* was a framed print. Medium-sized.

Soft silver wood.

Mondrian.

She stared. Her throat tightened.

"You talked about the balance," Clinton said, voice low. "How it made you feel grounded, I thought this space might need that too."

Her fingers stilled on the edge of the frame.

He stood just out of reach, fidgeting with the hem of his coat like this gesture had cost him something.

"A gift," she whispered.

His lips tilted. "Or insurance. Depends on how you frame it."

That earned a quiet breath of laughter.

She set the print gently on the wide windowsill, turning back to meet his stare.

"Thank you."

His shoulders eased.

She stepped toward him slowly, bare feet creaking across the cement. "You show up at inconvenient times with inconvenient truths and act like you're doing me a favor."

"I *am*," he said evenly, but the smallest curve touched his mouth.

Her fingers brushed his lapel. "We can't keep doing this halfway," she said. "You protecting me with paperwork while I pretend it's not personal."

"I'm not great at emotional boundaries."

She smiled crookedly. "That's obvious."

The moment expanded, thick with unspoken words.

Then, just as her hand fell back to her side, he stepped away.

"I should go," he said, voice too casual. "You need dinner. I promised takeout."

"You're leaving?"

"Just for now," he replied. "I think some distance is…smart."

He pulled the coat tighter, glanced once at the Mondrian, then left without waiting for her to reply.

The door clicked shut behind him.

Taylor exhaled. Slow. Unsteady.

She let out a long, slow exhale and stared at the framed print as if it might blink back.

Sometimes what people say to you says more than what they say out loud.

Sometimes it was easier to carry art than the truth.

She sat on the cool floor, surrounded by light, silence, and the echo of a man who cared more about her safety than her messiness.

She wasn't sure whether that scared her or made her want to show him how beautiful messy could be.

Chapter Twenty-One

Clinton

Clinton nudged the studio door open with his elbow, holding a bag of Thai takeout in one hand and a chilled bottle of wine in the other.

Inside, the setting sun streamed through the high windows in stripes, casting a dusky light over bolts of fabric and the beautiful chaos of progress. The space still smelled faintly of paint and time, but she'd lit a few candles and opened the windows, so now it smelled subtly like her.

"Dinner is served," he called gently.

Taylor looked up from the floor, one knee tucked under her, a pencil behind her ear. She was barefoot, wearing an oversized sweatshirt that slipped off one shoulder, surrounded by tangled sketchbooks and half-unwrapped silk.

Her smile appeared gradually. Not dazzling, but genuine. "You brought massaman curry, didn't you?"

"And drunken noodles," he said, crouching beside her. "After seeing this level of commercial-grade stress, carbs felt mandatory."

Taylor reached for the bag. "A correct assumption."

They unpacked dinner onto her largest table, which was technically an upcycled barn door balanced on painting blocks, and ate straight from the cartons. She picked out red pepper slices and dabbed a stray grain of rice with a paper towel.

"You're nesting," he said after a moment.

She froze, chopsticks mid-air. "Is that a diagnosis or a warning?"

"Just an observation. Thread scraps on the windowsill. Fabric sorted by color. A sketchbook with a coffee ring on it." He looked around. "This space is becoming something."

"Yeah," she said. "It is."

Then, more guarded, she said, "But nesting...that's a loaded word."

"You're building something new. Creating a home for it. Does that scare you?"

Taylor stared down at the curry for a beat, then shrugged. "A little, but mostly it feels like it's been waiting for me."

He held back a response.

She glanced up, cautious. "You're not going to tell me to scale back again, are you?"

Clinton set down his fork. "No. I've seen what you're building. I worry you'll put everything into this and forget there's more to protect than the idea."

Her jaw tightened. "Like what?"

"You."

She turned back to her plate, chewing more slowly. "You think I don't know that?"

"I think people who've had to survive get very good at working through exhaustion, and terrible at knowing when they're unraveling."

She didn't reply. Just began stacking leftovers in neat piles beside the wine glasses.

Clinton poured them each a drink. Handed hers over by the stem.

She took it, pinkie brushing his.

That light touch sparked something. All night, they hadn't really touched. Now, surrounded by the future she was sewing by hand, sitting under garish overhead lights softened only by the dusk-warmed windows, a single brush was enough.

They both paused.

Taylor shifted first. Her eyes dropped to his mouth.

"You keep looking at me like you're trying to talk yourself out of something," she murmured.

"Maybe I am."

Her gaze narrowed. "Why?"

"I think I owe you an apology."

She studied him. He couldn't tell if she was going to push him away or pull him in. At the very least, he'd been hurtful. At worst, he'd assumed she couldn't do this.

"You were trying to take care of me," she said finally.

He exhaled. "I just want you to be okay."

He set his takeout aside and moved toward her. "Sometimes I forget I don't have to fix everything, and I don't want to be the only thing keeping someone's life together."

"I don't need you," she said.

He nodded. "You do, but in the best way. You need support.

Affection. For someone to worship you, not control you. What you don't need is me second-guessing your every move."

She reached for his hand. "You're right. I do need that."

And then it broke the tension, the resistance, the kilometers of space they'd been carefully preserving. Taylor stood. Her bare feet were silent on the old wood floor, and she kissed him. No coy teasing. No room for second thoughts.

He sighed against her mouth and pulled her close. His hands slid along her thighs, skin warm through her leggings, and her sweatshirt bunching as her body melted into his.

The futon, her so-called fitting chaise, became their landing place, half-swallowed by satin bolts and laughter.

She kissed him as if he'd brought more than dinner, like he'd brought clarity.

He whispered something against the curve of her neck he hadn't meant to say aloud.

"Don't," she breathed, catching it. "Unless you mean it."

He met her eyes and didn't deny it.

Fabric pinned her legs and tangled with his. He was deliberate, steady, without hesitation in the way his mouth brushed her brow, her jaw, the hollow of her throat.

"You keep looking at me like I'm going to vaporize," she said.

"I just can't get enough," he replied.

No joke. No wink.

She reached towards the basket next to the futon, grabbed a blanket, and tucked it around them both, and curled in.

"They're going to tear into you," he whispered.

"I know."

"They'll want your brand. Your backstory. Your heart-break."

"I know."

"I just don't want to watch you get devoured."

"That's your job?"

He huffed a laugh. "Yeah, but—"

She was quiet for a long time, then she asked, "Sara?"

The name barely landed before the air shifted.

"I tried to love her through it," he said. "But she didn't want help. She wanted to prove she could do it alone."

Taylor bit her lip. "I'm not her."

"I know."

"You're not staying because you think I'll drown?"

"I'm staying because I want to build with you. Not rescue you."

She cupped his jaw. "I'm not bone china, Clinton. I thought I would crack, but I burned it all down and rose from the ashes."

He smiled, but it hurt. He'd loved a girl who'd been caught in the fire, but never one who became it.

Chapter Twenty-Two

Taylor

It started with a ping.

Taylor didn't check her phone right away. She'd been mid-drape, pinning a muslin overlay onto the dress form by the window, and humming along to an Ella Fitzgerald track playing low through the studio speakers. The sun was soft, filtered through linen curtains. She pushed up her sleeves and twisted her hair into a bun, securing it with clips and pencil stubs. There was silk on the table, her favorite espresso cooling beside her scissors, and for the first time in a while, hope had felt like a muscle she could flex.

Then the pings didn't stop.

Buzz. Buzz. Buzz.

Too frequent to be texts from Candy. Too rapid to be Bailey's usual string of curated updates. Taylor grabbed her phone.

The alert at the top of her screen buckled her knees.

FASHION WEEKLY: MYSTIQUE EXPOSED?

Plagiarized Paris? Fashion's Shiniest Mystery Has a Prob-

lem with the Past.

Below it was a photo.

The bronze carpet. Gala night.

A direct side-by-side comparison of one of Taylor's gowns and an older piece from Delacroix's Fall 2018 show. Hers looked bolder. Fresher, but the headline didn't say that.

It read: *Is She the Curator? Or a Copycat?*

And just beneath that, the pull quote: *"Sources suggest Taylor Rousseau's atelier may have borrowed brilliance from a collection curated years earlier."*

"No," Taylor whispered, the word snapping the quiet in half.

Another alert popped up.

Then another, and another.

Bailey: *I'm seeing it. Stay calm. Don't respond yet.*

Molly: *Fashion Weekly just pushed an alert. Their media team is asking if we have a comment. Don't give them one. Let me coordinate.*

Candy: *I will break his PR firm's windows. Say the word. I'll find a brick.*

Taylor's stomach twisted.

She opened Fashion Weekly's homepage.

Below the headline was a full write-up peppered with veiled accusations. *"Stylist sources say the designer behind Mystique is unproven. That her sudden rise mimics another, that elegant silhouettes and soft embroidery may not be original after all."*

The article referenced anonymous 'industry insiders.' It referred to similarity, not theft, but it didn't have to shout. The implication was clear. Taylor had taken designs she admired and pretended they were her own.

It even fueled the doubt Delacroix had likely seeded himself: "*Of course, no one could forget such a revolutionary silhouette. It debuted in his early Milan days. Was Mystique inspired by greatness, or just too close to call?*"

Her breath turned shallow.

She stepped back from the table, nearly knocking the espresso onto the floor.

Buzz.

Buzz.

Stylist 1: *Regretfully postponing fitting. Uncertain what the next steps will be.*

Stylist 2: *My client is feeling uneasy. We'll reach out when/if the story settles.*

Email. Text. Email. Phone call. Decline. Decline. Decline.

The phone vibrated in her hand; a number she didn't recognize flashed across the screen. For a split second, Taylor debated letting it go to voicemail. But instinct—or maybe hope—had her answering before she could think better of it.

"Hello, this is Taylor Rousseau."

A clipped, professional voice replied, "Taylor, this is Chloe Phillips. I represent the Rowlands. I wanted to speak to you directly."

Taylor pressed the phone tighter to her ear, heart tripping. "Of course. Is everything alright with the fitting? I sent over the final photos this morning. If they have questions, I'm happy to schedule another appointment—"

"I'm afraid it's not about that. We've seen the recent articles."

Taylor's stomach plunged. "Articles? You mean the Fashion Weekly piece? It's—look, I know how it reads, but none of it is true. If you'd like the story behind those sketches or references, I can provide whatever context you need. The Rowlands chose me, Chloe, not some headline."

A pause. The sound of shuffling papers. In the background, the muffled echo of another phone ringing in an office far away from anything Taylor could salvage.

Chloe's voice flattened. "The family is very sensitive to public perception, Taylor. I'm sure you understand the need for discretion in their relationships. While we admire your work, right now, any association with...well, with controversy isn't possible. If something changes and the situation settles, we'll reach out. Until then, we must decline further involvement."

Desperation bled into Taylor's words. "Chloe, please. This isn't a real scandal. If you give me ten minutes, I can show you the original sketches and timelines. This brand means everything to me. I wouldn't lie about someone else claiming my work, but I—"

"There's nothing to be gained by arguing, Ms. Rousseau. The Rowlands have made their decision. I'm sorry."

The finality in her tone struck Taylor like a closing door. Her mouth opened, then shut. There was nothing left to say.

"Thank you for your time," Chloe added, voice already gone cold. "I hope things improve for you. Goodbye."

The line went dead.

Taylor stared at her phone, hand shaking, no words left—only the echo of her client's withdrawal hanging in the quiet. The loss this time wasn't nameless. It had a voice and a deadline and nothing to do with design.

It felt surgical. Each article, text, and voicemail sliced away at a future she hadn't even lived yet, and all before lunch.

Taylor paced the studio, circling the wreckage of her ambition. Every surface showed the imprint of defeat. There were unfinished gowns slumped on dress forms like wilted petals, and the once meticulous rows of bobbins sat tipped and tangled near unused fabric skeins. Swatches littered the floor, bright scraps underfoot crushed by her restless path. She stepped over a spilled cup of chalk pencils, their dust smeared by frantic hands. Open pattern books fanned across the drafting table, pages creased from where she'd gripped them too tightly, searching for answers that wouldn't come.

The rolling racks she'd bought after her first rush of orders—sleek, sturdy, full of promise—were now mostly empty. The few hangers that remained twisted idly, bearing nothing but half-pinned mockups and hopeless muslins. They were hollowed-out proof that hope had once lived here and been chased out, rack by rack, by scandal.

Taylor's chest constricted as she took it all in. The floor was a minefield of discarded fabric, crushed patterns, and bunched thread. Each step threatened a fresh jab, a pin in her heel, a silent accusation she couldn't outrun.

A thousand questions spun through her mind, crowding out air. Had she fooled herself, thinking talent was enough? Had she ever really belonged at the center of all this shimmer and noise, or was she always meant to be overlooked—a cautionary tale about how high small-town girls with grand ideas could actually reach? The studio, once her sanctuary, now mirrored her unraveling; beautiful things, ruined by chaos, scattered too far apart to put back together.

She pressed a hand to her forehead, dizzy with the fear that maybe Laurent Delacroix had been right all along. Perhaps she wasn't a true designer. Maybe ambition was nothing more than arrogance dressed up in optimism, and the world was correcting her mistake. Every discarded cloth, every prick of a forgotten pin, whispered the same thing: *You should have known better. You should never have believed you could win.*

Taylor turned in the wreckage, pulse racing, jaw clenched to hold back grief. Another alert lit up the screen.

WORN Magazine: *Is Mystique a Mirage?*

She let the phone fall onto the worktable with a thud.

Tears burned behind her eyes, hot and helpless. Her hands shook. Her reflection—caught in the streaked old windowpane across the room—looked exactly like the vulnerable student she'd once been, standing frozen beneath fluorescent lights. At the same time, a professor asked why her best wasn't original enough.

She'd run before. Packed up her work. Filed it under 'Not Good Enough,' and buried it beside her name, and started over.

Now, here she was again. She choked back a sob.

Clinton.

She reached for her phone, paused—no new messages. The silence felt sharper than expected.

He was probably in a meeting, or with Bailey, or building a response plan, or reevaluating every moment of support he'd offered her. That thought sliced deeper than anything the internet could throw at her.

"Don't do this," she whispered, backing into the wall, both hands braced against the cool plaster. "Don't cry. He doesn't deserve any more of your energy. Do not give him this."

But it was too late. Her voice cracked. The tears she'd been batting back came in waves now—hot, frantic, unstoppable. She slid down, collapsed onto the studio floor in the narrow run of light beneath the skylight. The dusty glow made the space look holy. She felt anything but.

She was losing it.

Delacroix didn't need to prove she'd stolen anything. He only needed to make people believe she wasn't worth the risk. Already, the phone had stopped buzzing.

The silence was damning.

An unfinished gown slipped from a nearby dress form and puddled on the ground like trash. She reached out, knuckles brushing the silk before she yanked her hand back.

"That was mine," she said aloud, voice wet and bitter. "Every inch of it was mine."

Across the room, sketches fluttered from her drafting table, caught in the breath of a barely open window. Her sketch-book—the one Clinton had called a marvel—lay half-open on the floor like an afterthought.

Taylor curled her knees into her chest and stared at the racks she'd rushed to order. The ones she'd spun through weeks ago with champagne and friends and laughter in her throat.

All of it was slipping away.

Tears kept rising. She gave up trying to stop them.

Alone, surrounded by the quiet ghosts of her own ambition, Taylor whispered into the stillness. "Did I ever even stand a chance?"

No one answered.

Chapter Twenty-Three

Clinton

He was reviewing a disputed partnership agreement when his phone lit up with a news alert. The headline stopped him cold.

MYSTIQUE EXPOSED?

Clinton tapped the article open, jaw tightening.

A photo loaded slowly. It featured dramatic lighting, a bronze carpet backdrop, and Taylor dressed in one of her gowns, her expression partially hidden behind the mask she wore at the gala. Next to it, a carefully cropped Delacroix archive image from years earlier. There were different fabrics and subtler techniques, but just similar enough for speculation to latch onto the side-by-side comparison.

He scanned the article quickly. There were pull quotes, anonymous sources, stylists 'reconsidering relationships, whispers of 'reused silhouettes.'

He dropped his pen.

It wasn't an accusation.

It was worse.

The article was a slow-drip smear campaign. Shape-shifting innuendo designed to destabilize, erode confidence, and plant doubt without enough evidence to fight back. There was only enough evidence to raise doubts, but not enough to sue them for libel and win.

His gaze sharpened.

The phrases quoted "uncanny parallels," "unverifiable origin points," and "curious echoes." He had seen this before in boardroom takedowns. It was a PR assassination. This wasn't about truth. It was a surgical strike disguised as journalism.

No texts from Taylor. No emails or frantic calls. That didn't mean she hadn't seen it.

Only that the blast radius hadn't reached him yet.

He grabbed his phone and stood up fast.

The lease file for her studio sat open on his desk, still flagged at a clause he'd been checking. He closed it without looking, shoved his laptop into his bag, and stood frozen, trying to figure out what he should do.

Someone had struck the match.

And he didn't know if Taylor was already standing in the fire.

His phone buzzed. He looked at the display. *Candy.*
It's bad. She needs you.

Twenty minutes later, he was climbing the stairs to Taylor's loft studio, cursing every uneven riser and the lifetime of unspoken feelings sitting in his chest.

He hoped, perhaps foolishly, that maybe she hadn't seen it yet. Maybe she was still working, lost in sketches or silks.

But as soon as he stepped inside, he knew.

The space was a wreck. Fabric bolts tipped sideways, their ends unraveling onto the cement floor in soft, uneven trails where she'd dropped them. Pins lay scattered near one of the dress forms. Someone had pushed the sketch table back, not with care but frustration, and its edge was now pressed crooked against the wall. There was an unplugged iron tipped on its side, and a scorch mark bloomed beneath it. The smell of something faintly burned clung to the air.

Sheets of sketch paper had spilled across the studio like water. Most were loosely crushed, torn at the corners. Some were face down, others still visible, graphite lines smudged beneath heavy fingertips.

Even the light felt altered. The expansive skylight, once a source of warmth and clarity, let in a thin gray wash that made every unfinished hem and crooked needle look sharper than it should. In the quiet, the hum of the city barely reached—no music, no drafting pencil scraping, no gentle hum of a machine. Just breathe. Slow. Uneven.

And amid it all, Taylor sat—folded and still.

She sat back hunched, arms wrapped around her legs, with her chin resting on her sleeves. Her jacket hadn't entirely fallen from her shoulders, but it slid sideways, exposing one shoulder and the ridged tension in her posture. Her bun was undone in parts, strands falling against pale cheeks flushed raw, and her hands were empty.

Clinton stepped into the studio and stopped.

Her arms twitched slightly as if she might raise her head, then tightened instead around her knees. She didn't speak. Didn't move to hide. The certainty and poise he associated with her were gone. This was stillness, not by choice, but exhaustion.

He'd never seen her look so small before.

She wasn't just hurting.

She had disappeared into the hollow space where confidence used to live. He crossed the studio slowly. "I don't know if you want me here," he said quietly, "but I was worried about you."

No answer.

"I can get you food. Ice cream. Massaman curry?"

Still nothing.

He crouched. "Taylor?"

Her shoulders trembled just once. Like his voice cracked something open.

"I'm done," she said, voice thick.

She lifted her head.

Her face was blotchy, her eyes rimmed red, her hands trembling. No mask. No armor.

"I'm done, Clinton."

Not Clint.

He heard it like a slap.

She was curled up on the floor near the broken remains of the dress she'd abandoned, her body tense and folded inward. A journal she hadn't touched in weeks sat unopened beside her, its spine still curved as if it had fallen that way hours ago. Her own handwriting peeked faintly through the edge of the page, but she wasn't looking at it. She wasn't looking at anything.

Clinton sat beside her, careful not to touch her. Not yet.

"I can get cupcakes," he offered, voice low. "They aren't the same as Candy's, but it could help?"

Taylor's hair was coming loose in soft pieces, strands clinging to the edges of her damp cheeks. Lint from the floor spotted her leggings. A faint smudge of charcoal traced the inside of her wrist where she'd likely wiped at her eyes without thinking. Redness ran high across her cheekbones and temples, betraying the tears she'd tried to control.

She lifted her head as if it required effort she didn't want to spare.

The fire was missing from her eyes. Only the swollen rawness of someone who hadn't just broken, she'd been ground down, piece by piece, word by word. Her pupils were sluggish, lashes stuck together. Her mouth was trembling not from drama or anger—but from exhaustion. Everything Clinton had hoped she'd never feel again had found its way back to her.

You've already lost your voice once. Don't let him take it again.

He wanted to say it. He wanted to say so many things, but this wasn't a courtroom. This wasn't where he'd win by talking.

Clinton pulled in a breath and leveled his voice. "Well, it's official. I don't know what to do."

Nothing.

"I hate that you called me Clinton," he said. "That's how I know this is bad."

She flinched a little, but he saw it.

"To everyone else, I'm Clinton: suits and strategy. Filing cabinets and deadlines, but with you—" He paused, swallowing the lump in his throat. "I don't mind. I mean, I sort of like..."

Her breath caught, and she looked away.

He didn't stop. "You don't have to talk. You don't even have to believe me right now, but if you're in the dirt, I'm in it too. If this whole damn studio collapses, I will sit in the wreckage with you and build it back one nail at a time, because you're not allowed to disappear. Not like..."

Clinton's voice escaped him for half a second.

"Not like before," he said, quieter. "I saw what happened when someone gave up, and nobody caught them. You're not her. Taylor, I need you to let me be here before you push everything away."

The silence stretched thick and close between them.

Then, finally, her hand twitched—just barely—toward his leg. Not a touch. Not yet, but her fingers had moved.

Clinton stayed right where he was, voice low and steady. "You can fall apart. I'll hold the parts you're too tired to carry, and I swear, when you're ready, I'll help hand them back."

He waited.

In the quiet, she brought one shaking hand into her lap and turned it palm-up.

He reached out, warm fingers closing gently around hers.

It was a start.

"I lasted a little over a month," she said bitterly. "Made it through the gala, the fittings, three articles that called me a visionary...and now it's unraveling. I look too much like a man who's been stealing from me for years."

He didn't correct her. Didn't offer the headline's exact language. She'd seen it. He didn't need to say it aloud.

She looked at him, and something in his chest broke. The part of him that wanted protocol wanted to fix it with legal strategy and ironclad documentation, but what was happening here was personal.

"I tried," she whispered. "But maybe I'm not built for this."

"No," he said. "You're built *from* this."

She shook her head. "Finally, I thought, maybe now I belong. I'm tired, Clinton."

The way she repeated his name was too heavy, too distant.

"I don't know how to keep fighting when they're already writing the story without me."

He saw her, not as the woman who commanded rooms, but as the girl who once gave her best designs to a man who silenced her with a smile.

He could've mentioned contracts. Timelines. Strategy. Instead, he reached for her.

Clinton pulled her into his arms gently, like she might break if he wasn't careful. Her frame folded against his, and she let go. Quiet sobs soaked into the shoulder of his suit. She didn't disguise the noise, didn't apologize, didn't say a word.

He didn't offer solutions. He just held and anchored her.

The sobs hit hard and fast, soaking his shoulder. She didn't hide or apologize, and as he drew slow circles across her back, he realized with quiet, terrifying clarity: *He loved her. This couldn't end like it had with Sara.*

When Helen unraveled, no one saw it until it was too late.

And the fear that it could happen again—that he could lose Taylor too—burned hotter than anything he'd ever felt.

He looked down at her, sleeping now with her cheek pressed against his chest. She cried herself quiet. Her breath moved slowly and shallow, fingers still curled like she was bracing for another blow.

He tucked a length of thick fabric over them both and held her tighter, and all he could think, watching the shadows move across the ceiling, was: *What if I can't stop her from burning out?*

Because this wasn't just a job, she'd become stitched into the seams of his heart, and if she couldn't rise?

He wasn't sure he was ready to fall.

Chapter Twenty-Four

Taylor

From a corner booth by the window, Bailey waved Taylor over.

Taylor slid into the seat across from her, an oversized knit cardigan tugged tight around her shoulders like armor. Her hair was in a worn, low bun, and the faint smudges beneath her eyes hadn't disappeared in two weeks.

The café was warm and bustling, sunlight slanting through the tall glass windows, catching in the floating steam of espresso and the glare of the tin signs lining the walls. The morning crowd churned with the usual rhythm of pickup orders, slow-sipping regulars, quiet laptop tappers.

"You look like a country western song," Bailey said, pushing a cappuccino across the table.

Taylor let out a tired snort, then glanced out the window. "I look like someone who's been ghosted by a dozen stylists and one industry I thought was starting to tolerate me."

"You've been smudged, not erased," Bailey said.

Taylor didn't answer. She had just taken a sip of the cappuccino and let the silence settle between them.

Across the room, a burst of laughter pierced the noise. A man in a camel coat patted a friend's shoulder, their plates half-empty and sliding toward each other as an empty coffee cup teetered dangerously on the edge of their table. Nearby, a toddler in polka-dotted leggings knocked a juice box off her booster seat with a triumphant squeal. It hit the floor with a wet splatter, sending droplets of orange across the base of a chrome chair leg.

The barista's voice rose above the clatter. "Kenna! Large oat latte with caramel!"

Taylor sat slumping halfway into her chair, fingers curled around the lukewarm mug of coffee Bailey pushed towards her. The colors of the cafe were too bright, the laughter too thick at the edges. She watched it all through the fog settling behind her eyes, like she'd stepped behind glass and no one on the other side knew she was there at all.

"It's been two weeks," Bailey said, her voice softer now. "Two long, quiet weeks."

Taylor gave a ghost of a nod. "You can say it. I'm radioactive."

"You're unheard," Bailey corrected. "Everyone's waiting for things to settle. For a headline that softens the blow."

"I have no way to defend myself." Taylor stirred her coffee, chasing foam. "As long as he's saying I stole from him, a better headline isn't coming."

Bailey hesitated. Then, she reached into her leather folio and slid a slim sheet of paper across the table. A list. Short. Handwritten.

"What's this?"

"My smaller clients. Boutique-level. Not headline-chasers. Stylists who like getting in early. They don't care about a whisper campaign in Fashion Weekly; they want good design."

"And they can't afford to pay rumored prices," Taylor said, scanning the names.

"No," Bailey admitted. "But they can pay something. If things get tight, they might...keep the lights on."

Taylor didn't touch the paper. Just stared at it. "So that's the option. Smile, accept mediocrity, design in the background, and pretend it's enough again?"

"It's an option," Bailey said. "But not the only one."

Taylor leaned back against the booth, the noise of the café falling away as something in her expression shifted. Harder. Older.

"I thought I was building something real. I thought maybe, for once, I wasn't chasing scraps." She stared at the whipped heart the barista had pressed into her foam. It was soft, already melting.

"I believe in what you're building," Bailey said.

"I know." Taylor blinked slowly, hollow. "But belief doesn't pay rent."

Bailey folded her hands on the tabletop. "Before the gala, you were on fire. Stylists fought over your gowns; Influencers dropped your name like it was currency."

"And now?" Taylor's voice cracked, but only once. "Now I'm a cautionary tale."

Silence stretched, edged in sympathy.

"I've been thinking..." Bailey exhaled. "Molly and I were

talking…"

Taylor froze. She didn't need a push. Not anymore. "We tried your plan," she said. "I'm going back."

"To Serenity?"

She nodded.

"For good?" Bailey's voice softened.

"I don't know. Maybe." Taylor ran a hand through her bangs. "There's a rhythm there. One I can understand. No flashbulbs, no editorials. Just breathing room."

A pause.

Bailey hesitated. "And if something shifts? If the press dies down—"

Taylor didn't answer right away. She thought of Candy and Molly, of Candy's late-night "community check-ins" on Instagram, little posts that looked casual but always carried her name, and Molly's surgical rewrites of editor pitches, emails sent at midnight with notes that ended, *Don't reply. Just know you're not alone.*

Her friends had been holding her up without demanding thanks. If she had any peace left, it was because of them.

"Maybe I'll come back," she said at last. "Or maybe I won't."

Bailey swallowed hard. "Is this what you really want? Or is this just…safe?"

"Do you know what safe sounds like to someone burned out?" Taylor asked. "It sounds like a closed door and quiet mornings. It sounds like choosing peace, even if it means surrendering the dream."

Bailey stared at her for a long moment. "You know you

don't owe anyone your silence, right? Not Laurent Delacroix. Not the designers who turned on you. Not the ones who got scared the minute you demanded recognition."

"But I do owe myself a little bit of gentleness," Taylor said. "And I haven't been able to find that here."

Bailey reached across the table, covering her hand. "Then go get it. Just promise you'll call when you're ready to raise hell again."

Taylor managed a small smile. "You'll be the first to know."

They finished their coffee in companionable quiet.

Sometimes, finding peace was its own victory.

Even if it looked like going home.

Chapter Twenty-Five

Taylor

Taylor folded a bolt of deep emerald silk with a precision that felt ceremonial.

Her hands moved automatically to tuck, smooth, and stack while her chest rose and fell in slow, deliberate rhythm. The silence in her SoHo studio buzzed with endings. Light bled through the skylight above in quiet gray ribbons, catching the flecks of dust drifting through the air.

She glanced at the garment rack in the corner, half-empty now, save for a jacket prototype and the shell of a dress she'd never hemmed. She had boxed everything else or planned to leave it behind. A few donations. A few scraps. Her name was signed on the inside lining of dreams no one wanted to wear anymore.

The place felt like it was exhaling.

Her tablet buzzed somewhere under a pile of fabric swatches. The screen lit briefly—another text from Bailey.

She didn't read it.

Molly had sent one an hour ago, all caps: *WE'LL RE-BUILD.*

Candy had left a long voicemail about sugar cookies and the politics of forgiveness and what song she was going to force the bakery to play when Taylor walked back through the door. Something appropriately dramatic. Possibly Taylor Swift.

Taylor hadn't responded to any of them.

Not yet.

One more organizing burst, she promised herself. A few more drawers. One more shelf.

She carefully unpinned a string of color-coded threads from the corkboard she'd installed her first week here. They left tiny dimples behind--ghost holes where her confidence used to hang.

The shelves felt emptier now than when she arrived.

So did she.

Not that she regretted it, not all of it, but the leap, the risk, the gowns that shimmered like stories you'd never forget. There had been a moment before everything turned where she'd thought *maybe* all this could be hers.

But dreams at this altitude came with fierce winds, and if she fell, she wanted to land somewhere soft, somewhere like Serenity. There, failure came with casseroles and cautious optimism. Not cameras.

There, she'd remake her career on gentler terms. Maybe she'd start taking custom orders again. Maybe she'd stay anonymous until she didn't have to be anymore, or maybe she'd sit on the back porch of the boutique and remind herself who she was when no one was watching.

Taylor pulled open the bottom cupboard near the drafting

table. Three old portfolios tumbled forward, her LA-era work. She'd already gone through these weeks ago, before the gala, when the fire fueled her instead of burning her.

She flipped one open absently. Familiar pages. Sketches with her stubby, tiny handwriting, swatches clipped at the side.

She grimaced. They were simple lines, young, but solid.

Next. The same. Rough folder edges, graphite dust smearing into cotton weights, and annotations.

But the last one, the one she barely recognized from the cover, was stiff beneath her fingers.

She frowned. Pulled it free.

A navy softcover bound in cracked fabric. She rubbed the spine.

Odd.

This one hadn't been in the stack before.

She opened it.

Her heart stopped moving.

Inside, pages and pages of her old sketches, the paper heavier than she remembered, thick-grain cardstock frayed along the edges where her hands had worried the corners. She sat motionless for a breath, the entire room tilting until the light shifted, catching the faint sheen of graphite still vivid across the cream-colored pages.

This wasn't just her final collection.

These were her beginnings.

Explorations of fabrics pinned like relics to the margins. Sleeves shaped like waves, structured bodices softened by watercolor strokes in muted coral and ash blue. Ink bled through parchment in places where she'd gone too heavy on her pen.

And then she saw ink she hadn't put there.

Her pulse stuttered.

At the corner of one layout of silhouette number sixteen from her final semester, a bell-shaped sleeve sketch was a looping script.

Black ink. Neat. Familiar.

Her eyes scanned it, heart hammering louder with every word: *"Surprisingly mature palette. Note textile sourcing. Avoid over-embellishment."*

Then, a signature.

LD.

Her breath left her in a rush.

No, she blinked hard, thumb brushing the edge of the page. The ink had smudged slightly, just at the curve of the D, as if thumbed before it had fully dried.

She turned another page with hands that trembled.

"Structural awareness. Collar needs reworking, but the silhouette is better than expected."

Another annotation.

Another "LD."

Another place he had seen her.

She flipped again. Closer to the spine now, the pages soft from use. Laurent Delacroix's handwriting etched across the border in blue ink. He wrote in rigid and tidy block letters next to thumbnail silhouettes and fabric swatches. A boxy arrow pointed to a hemline with a scribbled *"ALREADY GOOD, TRY BROADER DRAPE?"* A hastily marked circle emphasized the dress collar profile. The ink had faded faintly in one corner and had bled slightly from humidity.

Page after page, her old designs appeared.

And then, a sticky note, pale yellow and curling at the corners, pressed between two pages. The adhesive had lost most of its grip years ago, so it floated loose as she flipped.

Written in his handwriting: *Promising. Archive these for the Spring board. Keep originals, especially the asymmetrical shoulder concept. LD.*

Her lungs knocked the air right out of her ribs.

He'd seen them and called them worth keeping, not in a classroom, not as feedback, not as part of any collaborative critique. He'd signed his initials as if they'd belonged to him.

She closed her eyes for a moment, pressing both hands flat on the weathered paper.

That was the piece he'd said he hated in her final review. She'd been so embarrassed she hadn't shared it with anyone, not even her peers, and here he was acknowledging that it was hers and that he liked it.

She ran her thumb along the margin and paused. A faint line of red pencil drifted over the lapel edge. That was Delacroix's feedback style: clean, measured, observational, more than inspired.

There were no notes of a mentor guiding a student; instead, they were a critic curating a collection.

"Oh my God," she breathed.

The sketchbook opened on its own now. Notes. Edits. Circles. Black slashes she remembered watching him make during studio reviews. Back then, they signified approval. Now they represented something else—evidence.

Her initials were scrawled in the back flap along with a

coffee stain and a half-ripped sticker from a long-forgotten boutique she used to frequent. She remembered tucking it between the others while moving out of her apartment.

How had she missed this with the other sketchbooks from Serenity?

Her gaze darted to the drawers Clinton had helped pack during the gala week fallout. She'd been too tired to look. He'd brought her boxes from home. Sketchbooks, folders, random bundles wrapped in her mother's old sewing patterns. Maybe it had been tucked into one of the old boxes. It was also possible that a seamstress had found it while digging for thread samples in her stash drawers and had put it here without saying a word.

She'd been too undone to notice. She hadn't opened this drawer since the day her world caved in two weeks ago, and now...this.

Pages of confirmation. Years of being gaslit and gutted pinned in his hand.

"No one knew," she murmured, voice uneven with disbelief. "Because I buried it."

She stared at the sketch with the embellished yoke and rose-flush satin details, the same one that had walked down the bronze carpet.

And there, in the corner, his note. Dated. Initials sharp-oiled in signature ink.

He'd seen them.

He'd signed them.

Now, she had time-stamped proof that she'd had the idea first.

The walls of the studio didn't move, but Taylor did. Her

heart began to lift through the grief strangling her chest. Her eyes burned with more than just exhaustion, and she reached for her phone.

When her fingers hovered over Clinton's name in her favorites, she didn't hesitate.

She tapped.

The phone rang once. Then twice.

When he picked up, she didn't bother to say hello.

"He saw them," she said, the words tumbling out like she'd been holding her breath all day. "He signed them, Clinton. He wrote in the margins. There's a note on the back of one, his handwriting, you remember those blocky capital letters? I have them. The sketches. From LA. I found them."

The line fell silent.

Then Clinton said, low and certain, "Is it dated?"

"Yes."

"Where was it?"

"I...I think it ended up packed with personal materials. I didn't even remember putting it there, but..."

"But you found it now," he said. She could hear him sit down. Paper shifting.

"This is the proof," Taylor said, voice hitching, awe creeping past the panic. "It's not just conjecture. It's not shared ideas. This is progression. Annotation. My line comes from this, and he literally signed on the page where it started."

Clinton's voice steadied into steel. "Then it's over."

Taylor sank to the floor, still clutching the portfolio to her chest.

Three words. Without meaning to, tears flooded her eyes.

"Clint," she said quietly, "It's not a feeling anymore. It's real. I can see it. I can hold it."

"Then justice starts now," he answered. "Keep everything exactly as you found it. Photograph it all, and, Taylor, get ready."

She nodded, even though he couldn't see it.

Her heart thudded hard in her chest, loud against the sudden stillness of the room.

This time, she wasn't going to let him rewrite her story, not again.

A slow sound reached her ears.

Her breath.

Shaking.

This. This was hers.

Evidence in hand, justice was finally within reach.

Chapter Twenty-Six

Clinton

Mahogany bookshelves lined the walls, their spines rubbed smooth by generations of scholars. Legal tomes stacked alongside aged whiskey bottles with labels turned deliberately away from view. They were both practical and an homage to Bailey's company, Ladder H Distilling, the company on which he built his reputation. The carpet beneath his low-heeled shoes was charcoal wool, barely a whisper against the rhythm of his steps.

But on his desk, anchoring the space like a fault line, was the sketchbook.

Not the original. He'd locked that in a fireproof satchel inside a sealed cabinet.

Clinton spread the printed pages he'd arranged, scanned, labeled, time-stamped, and watermarked before him as legal exhibits. He clipped them into a custom binder. Its matte black cover absorbed the afternoon light. He ran a hand over the edge, gripping the spine hard enough for his knuckles to show white. He was also aware of how familiar it felt to be on the brink of a fight, with evidence marshaled and arguments ready for the cold dance of litigation. The buzz of case prep now came with something raw and unprofessional gnawing at the center of his chest.

He stared at the exhibits filled with sketches and fabric swatches, annotations in Delacroix's careless hand, the quiet precision of Taylor's work made visible alongside proof of its theft. He'd built a career on gathering facts, imposing order, and controlling narrative with paperwork and precision. Usually, he felt steady here. Invincible. This time, the more he looked at Taylor's portfolio, the more personal this became. She was not just any client. She was not paperwork, a puzzle, or a cautionary tale. This was the woman whose quiet courage had pressed color into the gray spaces of his well-defended life, whose losses felt suddenly like his own.

He picked up a page and turned it slowly between his fingers, letting the weight of it settle. The evidence was solid: timelines, annotations, original sketches bearing both her signature and Delacroix's commentary. A judge would see it. Even a hostile judge would see the evidence, but he couldn't guarantee justice, and fear made him wonder: *what if the facts weren't enough?* What if the world clung to spectacle and rumor instead of the truth?

He pressed a thumb to his jaw, grounding himself. He'd seen what happened when people lost their voices. Sara's memory still tempted him to retreat, to choose safety over hope. Taylor wasn't Sara. She didn't want anyone to rescue her. She needed someone to believe in her enough to help her fight, and to stand by her if it all went wrong. That was what mattered.

Not simply winning, but witnessing. Defending her, not managing the risk.

He took another slow breath and straightened the binder. This wasn't just about strategy anymore. It was about Taylor walking through the world untarnished, her name restored, her story anchored publicly to her own creation. It was about making sure she never crouched in the shadows again, forced to watch someone else collect applause for her scars and her labor.

He imagined what came next. There would be a call to Bailey, a flurry of messages to Molly and Candy, legal memos stacked with press releases and NDAs, coordinating every moving part so that, this time, no one would rewrite Taylor's story but her. He saw Taylor at the center of it all, head held high, finally taking back ground she should never have lost. He was about to set every piece in motion, and for once, the outcome would matter for reasons that had nothing to do with his career or ambitions. Perhaps she'd finally believe he was in this with her, not just for her.

With a last glance at the evidence—his proof, her redemption—Clinton exhaled and rolled his shoulders beneath his pressed shirt, feeling the crisp starch strain and settle under the tension flowing through him. The line between courtroom and heart might be a fine one, but it was the only battle he wanted to fight.

He reached for his phone, throat tight, not from nerves or tactics, but from hope, ready to make the call that might change everything.

He scrolled without hesitation.

Bailey.

Her name blinked back in soft, bold lettering.

Three rings.

"You're calling me twice in one week," Bailey said instead of hello. "So. Either somebody's dead, or this is a personal call."

"Taylor found something," he said without buildup. "An old Sketchbook from LA with his notes."

Silence.

He could imagine her sitting down at the table in her farmhouse kitchen, probably pushing Rosie's macaroni art off a folder to make room for the gravity of what he'd just said.

"She has proof," he continued, voice low and firm. "Initialed by Delacroix. Comments in the margins. It's dated. Scanned. I verified the paper grade and markings—everything aligns with the timelines. This is the thread that unravels his entire defense."

A slow breath on the other end. "She told me she'd packed up."

"She's still packing," he said. Then, softer, "But I don't think she wants to leave. Not really."

"Clint—"

"I'm calling in the favor. You said after the gala...whatever I needed."

"I remember."

"I need you to stall her. One day. Just give me that."

He sat down behind his desk. For once, he didn't straighten the folders or calculate his words for maximum precision. He just ran his hand through the dark line of his hair, mussing it for the first time in hours.

"Keep her in the city long enough for me to show her who

she really is," he said. "Not what the headlines say. Not what he stole."

Bailey was quiet for a long time.

"You're planning something, aren't you?"

"I'm always planning something."

"But this time, it's personal."

"Yes." His voice gentled, threading past the legal formalities. "Because I don't just want to win back her reputation. I want to give her back the woman she buried when she ran from LA."

Another silence. Then the steel in Bailey's tone curved into something warmer. "You really love her."

"I didn't mean to," he said, voice barely above a hum. "But yeah. That's the sort that sticks."

Bailey exhaled. He could almost hear her smile.

"Then tell me what you need."

He looked down at the open binder. The sketches stared back at him; genius patched together with grit and thread and ink. Her legacy. Her proof. Most importantly, her voice.

For a moment, the familiar rhythm of trial prep tried to reassure him. This was his world—evidence sorted by tabs and highlights, a cascade of legal points stacking up to make a case airtight. The stakes here felt nothing like the dozens of corporate battles he'd fought before. As he traced Taylor's clean pencil lines, her signature faint at the margin, Delacroix's blocky notes like graffiti on a cathedral, Clinton felt the hairs rise along his arms.

He wasn't just stewarding a win; he was protecting Taylor's very core, and it gutted him how much he wanted the world to witness her victory.

By the time he ended the call, the blueprint for redemption had already begun to unfold, not on a neat timeline, but in a knot of hope, strategy, and fear. His mind whirled. This wasn't the measured calculation of a closing argument; it was the desperate, terrified drive of a man who knew he had one shot to help the woman he loved take back her own story.

He clicked over to the shared spreadsheet Molly had built. Molly's spreadsheet included color-coded campaign tiers, Influencer availability, and pre-approved third-party legal commentators. Candy's notes spilled over into the margins in a riot of fonts and smiley faces. He should've been annoyed, but the chaos was comforting. Taylor's friends rallied with the same urgency knotted in his chest.

He thumbed through the finalized documents one last time checking gifting clauses to protect Taylor's IP in every upcoming partnership, sworn statements from stylists who'd witnessed her creative process, screenshots archiving early emails and receipt dates, and the first draft of Molly's anonymous press piece about "the real origin of this season's most controversial silhouette."

A bead of sweat trailed down his collar. He wiped it away, throat tight with anticipation, and dialed his assistant.

"Push all my calls," he snapped, voice low. "I need copies of these NDAs to every participating stylist by noon, no leaks until I approve every last signature. Could you bring me a coffee? The strong stuff."

Clinton scrawled a to-do list across his legal pad, hand barely steady: Press plan, Influencer embargoes, call Jackie at The Times, triage the social media strategy, and organize the order of the Mystique pop-up so that Taylor's originals and Delacroix's annotated versions would be side by side on projection. He needed the crowd stunned by the evidence before Laurent Delacroix could poison the narrative again.

He hit speed dial for Janelle, a PR bulldog who owed him a favor and could whip press sentiment with a single tweet, leaving a detailed voicemail about embargo timings, exhibits release, and Influencer seating. He texted Molly: *Find one more stylist to slip behind the scenes. Organic first, media circus second.*

Clinton made himself still for a beat, staring at the binder, letting the adrenaline sizzle in his veins. He ached to jump in his car, race across the city, and hand Taylor her victory in person. He forced himself to work the plan, to honor the strategy she deserved.

Calls. Contracts. Outreach. All of it was for her.

He was impassioned, almost wild. His heart thudded with desperation. It had been years since he'd wanted something to work this much, and it terrified him. He was confident in the details, certain of the law, but inside, he was as raw as Taylor had been the night he first saw her destroyed on the studio floor.

He flipped through the binder's exhibits one last time, took a deep breath, and started dialing.

This was what it meant to champion someone. Not just to win, but to make sure the world understood exactly who she was. Clinton was not going to let anyone—not Delacroix, not a headline, not even a shadow of a doubt—rewrite the truth again.

It wasn't just a case file.

It was a reckoning.

This time, he wasn't just shielding her from impact; he was helping her step into the light.

When everything was packed, Clinton straightened his tie, grabbed the garment folder and USB with scanned evidence, then looked out across the city skyline, deepening into early evening.

Then he left to win her back.

Taylor answered the door in bare feet wearing paint-splattered joggers, one side of her hair pinned up and the other falling forward in a spill of silver-touched brown curls.

The sketchbook sat open on her table, proof in margins and ink, but her eyes looked wary, as if the disbelief hadn't thoroughly worn off yet.

"You're still here."

"Bailey pushed my flight to tomorrow. I guess there's some plumbing issue at the shop."

He sent up a silent thank you for the favor fulfilled and held out the bag he was holding. "I brought dinner."

"You realize you don't have to bribe me with dumplings anymore." Taylor lifted a brow.

"I wasn't sure where we stood," he admitted. "But it felt safer to feed you anyway."

She stepped back. "Come on in."

The table was already cleared, and a candle flickering low beside her planner. He set the file folder down carefully and took her hand gently, as if she might still change her mind.

"I know you weren't sure about fighting again," he said. "But I am. Not just because I love you, but because the world is starving for something real. What you built...what you made...it matters."

"You love me?" she asked, the words nearly inaudible.

He didn't look away. "It's been coming for weeks. Every time you adjust a sketch with a frown, it means you are on the edge of genius. Every time you handed me tea instead of coffee and assumed I'd had too much caffeine. Every moment you challenged me to believe in you, even when you didn't believe in yourself."

"Clint, I haven't given up, I just...moved too fast."

"Sure, you were reckless and a little impulsive, but you have something Helen didn't have...humility. You know your limits and what you're capable of doing. You lack confidence, but you appear to have borrowed some of that, this time, from the enigmatic group of women you call friends."

"They are pretty special."

"They are, and everyone believed in you. Your dress is in a museum! You made a mark, but you lost confidence in yourself, again. Now, it's time for you to shatter the rest of the walls holding you back."

Emotion hit her fast. She blinked but didn't step back. "What did you do?"

"I made preparations for your last stand."

He opened the folder. Walked her through it. Contracts. Statements. Strategy. Everything they would need not only to win the legal fight with Laurent Delacroix, but to reclaim the story clawed from her hands.

"And if I say yes?"

"Then tomorrow, the campaign goes live. Anonymous leaks. Visual corroboration. Testimonies. A press thread no one can ignore. You'll debut again, this time with your own name. No masks. Just proof."

"What if I'm scared?"

He stepped closer, lifted a single curl from her cheek. "Then you remember your runway training and walk forward anyway, and I'll be right there with you."

She shifted towards where he sat on the futon and kissed him gently, not slowly. Hungry. Certain. It was a kiss that stripped every what-if from the room and replaced it with yes, and now, and yours.

Light spilled across her shoulder from the window's haze—tea-colored, aching with dusk.

"You're so damn beautiful," he whispered.

"I know," she whispered back, smiling as his lips found the soft skin just below her collarbone.

Then softer. "And I love you."

He stilled, but only for a second.

Then she looked up at him, eyes clear in the lamplight's glow, voice rooted.

"I love you," Taylor said again. "Not just for your gentle nurturing or your strategy sessions. Not because you fixed any of this, but because you never asked me to be anything less than who I am." She softened then, her fingers curling into his jaw like she was memorizing the shape of this moment. "Even when I didn't know who that was, or you were worried it might be too much."

Clinton's eyes shimmered. "I've loved you," he murmured. "Since the minute you called me Clint, and I couldn't wait until you said my name again."

He kissed her then—less hungry this time.

More reverent.

He kissed her as if he were stitching her back together with his mouth. Like every inch he touched was a sacred vow made breath and skin.

Clinton brushed a lock of hair from her cheek.

"We'll face it tomorrow," he murmured.

"But tonight?" She asked, tracing the edge of his collarbone with the softest part of her fingertip.

"Tonight, we hold it close."

He shifted beside her, adjusting until she was nestled against his chest, his arm beneath her neck, her palm resting at the base of his throat. Reassuring. His breath was steady.

Somewhere in the background, her phone chimed again. It was probably Bailey or Molly. A headline, maybe, but Taylor didn't move.

She was right here.

Wrapped in the arms of a man who loved her as fiercely as he protected her, with her name no longer hidden, her worth no longer doubted.

The city pulsed quietly beyond the glass.

But here, in a tangle of limbs and blankets and candlelight that had dimmed to a soft gold, Taylor and Clinton held each other through the quiet.

Just being.

Chapter Twenty-Seven

Taylor

The pop-up show wasn't on the map—literally.

No signage. There were no addresses on the invites. Just a cryptic location pin dropped into private inboxes and a teaser caption posted by handpicked fashion darlings: *Tonight only. Chelsea. Mystique revealed.*

Inside Taylor's Chelsea studio, what was once a quiet workspace built from vintage bolts and secondhand drafting tables now buzzes like the backstage of a Paris runway. Muslin runners weave between mirror-lined partitions lit from behind, softening the natural planked wood floors that are swept and polished. Ring lights flicker to life near the far wall, casting an editorial glow across the makeshift runway.

Under the dim lights, they'd transformed the studio.

Sleek black mannequins replaced dress forms on custom risers. Violet tulle and emerald silk decorated the walls. Edison string lights hung from the rafters, reflecting off vignettes of scattered glassware and vintage crockery layered with painted sketches and half-eaten macarons in blush and gold.

Flutes of rosé and lime soda clinked in clusters of stylists dressed like they'd stepped out of a spread. On the overhead speakers, a playlist pulsed with the low throb of cello.

Molly stood mid-floor, walkie-talkie clipped to her waistband, gesturing in sharp angles as volunteer models lined up near the wall. Their dresses shimmered in silk, tulle, crepe, and organza—stormy tones and sunlight pastels.

Candy bustled near the folding table rebranded as catering, laying out her signature hors d'oeuvres on vintage stands. "Help yourself to a treat. We have button cookies, sew good brownies, and thimble mousse cups," she declared, waving a spatula at a passing photographer. "Get a beauty shot. I piped the rosettes by hand."

Bailey, with two phones and a tablet, waved over her most trusted Influencers and New York society darlings. "Remember," she murmured, handing out sleek black masks, "this is about authenticity. Show elegance, show edge, but most importantly, show what Mystique is capable of."

At the far end, a towering curtain concealed a screen the width of the wall. Only Molly had seen the final version of what would play. She'd launch it on Clinton's signal.

"We've got twenty-five minutes," she called, checking her clipboard. "Taylor, final confirmation?"

Across the room, Taylor stood near the lineup, clipboard in hand. She wore tailored black slacks and a sleeveless cowl-neck top in soft taupe, the fabric folding over her collarbone and knotted just above her waist. A gold cuff glinted on her wrist, narrow heels peeking beneath her hemline. Nothing screamed.

It all whispered confidence.

Behind her, models stood in staggered rows like living exhibits, draped in silk, linen, and tulle, their neutral palettes kissed with rose-gold. Shoes lined the floor like punctuation. A tilted mirror reflected the chaos of final touches—zippers zipped, hems pinned, powder dabbed at collarbones.

Overhead lights bathed it all in a champagne glow.

In the far corner, Clinton stood near the double doors in charcoal slacks, a white shirt rolled at the sleeves, and no tie. Relaxed, but alert. A watchful stillness. He hadn't looked away from her since arriving.

Taylor looked up, clipboard resting on one elbow. Her eyes scanned the room for spacing markers, cue signals, and soundtrack levels.

Their eyes locked.

No smile. Just a lift of her chin and a single nod.

"Confirmed," she said, voice low but certain. "We're ready."

Clinton didn't move. His hands stayed tucked in his pockets. There was nothing left to fix.

At the cue, the studio doors swung open.

A surge of people followed. Press murmurs rose. Stylists lifted phones discreetly. Shutters clapped like applause. Influencers lined the gallery's edge, lanyards glinting under sharp light. The air shifted—tense, reverent.

Draped ivory voile had transformed the walls, which were lined with archival sketches and cloth-bound journals hanging between smoked glass panes. Behind it all, the giant projection screen stayed still. Blank.

Then, from behind a velvet partition, Taylor stepped out.

She exhaled and lowered the clipboard. No retreat. Just forward.

Guests moved like smoke through the space. No heels clattered. No bodies jostled. Just murmurs. Skeptics in eucalyptus wool, editors adjusting cufflinks, artists eyeing color choices. Restraint reigned, but brows lifted. The air hummed, quiet, but ready.

Molly stood near the entrance, in slate blue satin and silk piping. Clipboard gone. Eyes calm.

"Tonight," she said, "we present Mystique's unreleased capsule collection. It is personal. Uncompromised. Completely her own." She raised hand-pressed envelopes, each wax-sealed with an M. "Inside is a QR code. Scan for exclusive access. Tonight is a closed ecosystem—no tags, no sharing—until the last look."

The crowd accepted it. They already knew this wasn't for Instagram. It was for witnessing.

Bailey moved through the offstage section, adjusting necklaces, checking hems, whispering behind sleek pinned hair.

"That bodice is perfect."

"Shoulders tall. You're art, not afraid." She grounded herself, prepared to act as a conductor behind the curtain.

Nearby, Candy balanced trays in one arm, passing a lime spritz with the other. Eyeliner sharp, sneakers dusted in glitter. "This isn't just fashion, it's theater," someone whispered.

Candy tipped her glass. "A show you'll never forget."

The music shifted. Lower. A cello bow scraped, weighty and slow.

Lights dimmed. Once. Twice. Stillness swept the room.

A swell of synth and glass harmonica. Then the first model stepped out.

She wore a bronze gown cut like molten metal. One shoulder was bare, and her skirt was tiered asymmetrically. Delicate beading traced the waist like constellations. Her hair slicked back, makeup bare except for gold-leaf eyes painted in quiet defiance. Nothing borrowed. All Taylor. Behind her, the screen flickered to life.

Side by side was a sketch in graphite lines with Taylor's handwriting in the margins, and the final gown. Process and product. Muse and manifestation. *Proof.*

The crowd leaned forward.

Model two rounded the corner. Another sketch flickered along with her dated sketches. Then, a Delacroix photo from two years ago. Same lines. Same hem, but beneath them was her date stamp.

By model four—wearing the butterfly collar—every editor was leaning in.

Clinton stood beside the screen, arms folded. He wasn't watching the clothes. He was watching them see the truth.

"She signed those sketches in 2014," someone murmured.

"Why was she hiding?" one Influencer whispered.

The room buzzed with the charge of something real.

The music dipped. Then rose.

Silk and velvet spilled over sharp heels. Architectural collars. Pleated skirts. Sleeve details like sculpture. The models moved with restrained elegance. Fabrics whispered like secrets, light catching in all the right places.

With each look came proof projected side-by-side with

Delacroix copies. Hems mirrored. Strokes duplicated. Necklines reimagined, but still obviously hers. The audience didn't gasp. They stilled.

Molly manned the slides. Bailey watched, arms crossed, lips pressed.

Candy, halfway through her champagne, broke the silence with her Southern rasp. "Who knew Mystique was this hot?" Her voice cracked. "I mean...look at that hemline." Then louder, "Strike. The. Pose."

The model did—chin tipped, stiletto forward, asymmetric drape lit by stage lights.

Molly nodded. "Cue the last move."

Taylor stepped onto the runway.

The room erupted.

She didn't wave. Didn't speak. Just walked. Wearing the same gown she'd made for the gala, but this time, unmasked.

Taylor Rousseau wasn't Mystique now.

She was the originator.

Phones rose. People called her name.

Molly fired a quote to The Times: *MYSTIQUE REVEALED. And the truth? Elegant as hell.*

Taylor reached the end of the walk and turned beneath the lights.

The screen behind her flickered: *ART IS CONNECTION. CONNECTION IS OURS. STYLE ISN'T OWNED. IT'S CLAIMED.*

Below that: *TAYLOR ROUSSEAU / DESIGNER. CREATOR. OWNER.*

The cheer was thunderous.

Applause rose in waves, flashbulbs flared, the air shimmered with heat and momentum.

Taylor stood centered, her gown trailing like smoke. Her hands trembled. The gown hugged her. The high collar, structured shoulders, and a lining stitched to her embrace her body with the same words she once whispered into shadow-dresses.

For you. Not for the world.

But this?

This was both.

Voices rose. Chanting, first scattered, then steady. Her name.

Not Mystique.

Taylor.

Bailey, her eyes glassy, pressed her hand to her lips. Candy didn't bother hiding her tears, mascara streaked, brownie in hand, slapping someone's arm with joy.

Molly lifted her phone, voice low with pride. "Told you she was a star."

On the edge of it all, Clinton moved. Tie loosened, stride steady. He didn't look around. Instead, he focused only on her.

Taylor turned before he reached her, summoned by something unspoken. The crowd, the cameras, the chaos, and it all fell away.

She met his eyes and didn't look down.

He reached for her hand, and she gave it freely. Fingers laced. Palms pressed. Clinton lifted their joined hands.

The cheer doubled.

Flashbulbs burst, and the room echoed with the name that mattered most...*Taylor Rousseau.*

Not muse. Not myth.

Herself.

She stood in the light and claimed it all.

Chapter Twenty-Eight

Taylor

The shift in the studio was sudden.

The applause faltered. Conversations stuttered mid-sentence. Even the low thrum of cello music seemed to catch its breath as the door swung open and Laurent Delacroix strode inside.

Gasps spread like falling dominoes.

He moved quickly, shoulders tense, eyes alert. His suit fit him with deadly precision. The man wore matte black wool with a sharp, angular cut that sliced at the sides, pressed with ruthless accuracy. The sheen of his lapels caught the overhead light like a blade, but it wasn't the clothing that took your breath away. It was the fury etched into the clean lines of his face. No mask this time—just raw, unveiled anger.

He looked like something boiling beneath velvet.

The room, still fragrant with citrus cocktails and warm fabric starch, exhaled as one and folded instinctively to make space. An aisle cut sharply down the center of the studio. Stylists stepped backward. Bloggers froze mid-comment.

Delacroix's polished shoes struck the floor. Each step echoed louder than the one before. His breath hitched, fast but measured, pulling through his nose like it hurt him not to scream aloud. Buttons on his cuffs gleamed like polished obsidians. Not a crease out of place. He wore his fury the way he wore his tailoring—tight, crisp, unforgiving.

He stopped three strides from the base of the display platform, spine rigid. Delacroix didn't need a microphone. Rage, when wielded so precisely, carried well enough.

"You dare," Delacroix spat, the words dragging razor wire through every syllable, "Parading my work in front of the press like it was yours to claim?"

His voice cut through the hush like a snapped wire. Sharp enough, someone in the back dropped a stemless wine glass. It didn't shatter. It just rolled into silence.

A hundred phones rose like lighters at a stadium concert. Videographers whispered into lapel mics. Editors craned their necks, pens ready, eager to write the confrontation headline before the tears could even fall.

Taylor stood at the far end of the runway platform.

Mid-conversation with a stylist from Milan in shoulder pads sharp enough to double as sculpture, her posture had been relaxed just seconds earlier, shoulders down, foot just slightly turned, mouth open in that familiar tilt she wore when describing a hem curve or a panel tuck. Now, the stylist was melting backward in slow reverence.

One step, two. Making room.

Taylor didn't follow her. She didn't retreat. Didn't bow.

Her silhouette still held the afterglow of triumph.

Her gown was pale ash-purple tonight, with a bias-cut hem trailing behind like poured moonlight. The modest collared bodice appeared regal. Her earrings glinted steady brass, vintage, pulled from her boutique long before the whispers of Mystique had found traction. Her hair, once curled softly around her jaw, was now swept into a braided crown. Loose enough to look elegant, but secure enough to look unbothered.

She looked up, but not down.

Delacroix's breath hitched.

Across the room, Clinton moved. One hand slipped off his pocket, the other shifting instinctively toward hers—a quiet reflex honed by months of tension, loyalty, and something deeper he barely let the room see.

His lawyer's stride wasn't frantic, just loaded. Prepared. Protective. His jaw set. Shoulders squared.

But the moment before their fingers touched, Taylor lifted a single hand.

Graceful. Unshaking.

Just a calm, deliberate gesture.

Not for Laurent Delacroix.

For Clinton.

A signal. A boundary. A choice.

Her fingers curled subtly enough to say, *I see you.*

Her chin tipped upward, and she turned her head just enough to catch his stance in the corner of her eye. There was no apology in it.

She didn't have to say, *"I don't need you."* Because her eyes already whispered, *I've got this.*

Clinton, trained to argue, to defend, to stand between impact and consequence—stilled. He dropped his hand.

The studio's overhead lights caught on the curve of Taylor's cheekbone and the fine black stitching along the collar of her custom suit. Her heels, matte charcoal and razor-sharp, clicked as she turned fully toward Delacroix, grounding herself into the cool, polished cement. Behind her, the projection illuminated her silhouette in amber and frost—like sunrise cracking open through glass.

The screen shimmered with her archived sketches in graphite and charcoal, her notes inked in deliberate swoops across cream paper, and spelled in full caps above the proof: TAYLOR ROUSSEAU | DESIGNER. CREATOR. OWNER.

She took a breath, then she spoke. "You've spent the last decade polishing a lie," she said, her voice steady and measured. "Smiling for cameras and using my designs when your talent ran dry."

Taylor stepped down slowly from the platform, the crowd silent except for the low thrum of the cello still echoing distantly overhead.

Each click of her heels echoed, purposefully. Deliberately. Her column suit moved with her like armor reimagined in bias stretch and edge-stitched justice.

"And the worst part?" she continued, stepping closer, her sash brushing her side like punctuation. The room leaned forward en masse, a sea of held breaths and clenched jaws. "The worst part was how easy it was for you to make me doubt myself. How easy it was for you to rewrite my name into a footnote while the world painted you the genius."

Laurent Delacroix flinched. Just slightly. "I didn't take anything from you."

Taylor didn't answer. Not immediately. Instead, she stepped to the side and raised the small remote Clinton had placed in her hand earlier.

Click.

Behind her, the projector clicked gently to the next slide.

The image changed.

A page of cream cardstock, layered in graphite, filled the screen. A sleeve cut in elliptical angles. Her signature half-circle hem. Right there beneath a sketch was a note.

LD – Has merit. Keep for future spring concept.

The audience inhaled in tandem, a rustle of expensive fabric and stunned disbelief.

Taylor turned back to him, her words softer now, quieter.

"You took everything," she said. Barely above a whisper but cutting sharper than any shout. "And then you built your empire pretending it came from you."

Another sketch appeared behind her—the same design he'd debuted three seasons ago in Milan, reshaped, repainted with silk, but unmistakable in its origin.

Delacroix stiffened, his posture torn between performance and retreat.

"I built a legacy," he bit out. "You drew some pretty pictures."

His voice barely carried over the rustle of cameras, but Taylor didn't look away.

"No," she said. "I made art. I made woman feel beautiful in

their bodies, again. You tried to steal that."

She matched his height with her precision, not her volume. "I was the girl who believed in approval more than herself, and you fed on that. You saw brilliance and claimed it as your own."

The following image loomed. Another sketch. Another annotation. The side-by-side composition features her early textile notes, annotated in archival ink.

Delacroix's jaw worked tight.

He laughed, sharp and dry. Pure defense. "You think Instagram likes and a few anonymous blog posts will change the reputation I've built?"

Taylor didn't blink. Instead, she clicked the remote again. This time, high above the platform, the screen dissolved into a carousel.

One by one, each slide grew bolder with sketches, fabric notes, and side-by-side comparisons from his own collections.

Each frame flashed with one glaring truth: *They were her design, with his name on them.*

The crowd murmured and churned.

A rising chant followed: *Taylor. Taylor. Taylor.*

But she didn't turn toward them, only back to him. "To anyone who questioned me, I have nothing to prove," she said. "But to every woman who's ever been told her gift needs a louder voice to matter—this is what reclaiming looks like."

He flinched again. This time, visibly.

Clinton stepped forward two paces, then stopped. She didn't need him now. This was hers.

The slide changed again, and the crowd surged into applause. Not polite. Not congratulatory. *Explosive.*

#MystiqueNoMore

TAYLOR ROUSSEAU | DESIGNER. CREATOR. OWNER.

And finally, flashing in a cloud of gold overlays:

#RousseauNotDelacroix

Delacroix's phone buzzed. He drew it from the interior pocket of his tailored jacket, his fingers still curled with residual tension. The screen lit against his face. He hesitated. A hush fell across the crowd, not because anyone could hear the message, but because everyone wanted to know what he would do next.

His brows pulled together, slow and feral, as if resisting whatever was waiting at the other end of that glow.

He glanced down. One line. A message from his legal counsel.

STATEMENT WITHDRAWN.

No fanfare. No apology. Just two words that slipped the dagger between his ribs with surgical accuracy.

He exhaled sharply through his nose. Not a sigh. Something meaner. Emptier.

His posture caved inward, barely perceptible, like the breath had been punched clean out of him. The muscle in his jaw twitched. His shoulders, always held like sculpted stone, sagged half an inch. Not enough for the press to call it defeated, but enough for everyone watching to know the armor had cracked.

He looked up once more, scanning for support among the crowd.

No one met his gaze.

Not the stylists hovering near the edibles table. Not the editors still clutching their phones like lifelines. Not even the fellow designer he'd once mentored, now fidgeting with his collar a few feet back, eyes full of sudden, selfish doubt.

No one followed.

The crowd didn't part for him this time. He had to step wide around the debris of his own vanity. The man was tight-shouldered, silent, and scorched by the spotlight he had once welcomed like divine right.

As he turned, a little too fast, the fall began in earnest.

His hand brushed the edge of a vintage chair beside the aisle, and he righted it with deliberate precision. A man still playing for dignity. Still performing the part of the untouchable titan, but he narrowly missed the chair's leg. It tilted, scraped the floor with a wooden groan, and stilled.

So did the room.

That sound—tiny, seismic—echoed louder than anything he said aloud, and that was when they looked past him.

Not around. Not through. *Past.*

They turned, column by column, row by row, drawn to the center again. To her.

Taylor.

Still poised at the head of the runway platform. Still under the golden spill of overhead lighting that haloed her hair and threw a soft glow across her low-bowed shoulders. She wasn't merely illuminated by the stage setup anymore. She was the light source.

Taylor inhaled. A deep, even breath that coasted through her shoulders and down the long, fluid line of her spine. Her gown shifted as she moved. The final slide, her signature, her claim, flickered behind her, washing the space in soft ivory tones.

Camera lenses tilted up.

Phones lifted.

All of them captured the moment as her heel clicked once more against polished cement, one single, grounded step forward.

Chin up.

Mouth relaxed.

Eyes fierce, but unburdened.

Her gaze didn't follow Delacroix's retreat. She refused to let him steal one more second.

Because this was her moment.

The echo of her name burst out from the crowd again. Louder this time. A rhythmic chant with no permission asked and no hesitation granted.

"Taylor."

"Taylor."

"Taylor."

And finally, she believed it.

Taylor Rousseau.

She took the final step to the edge of the platform and paused. Head high. Shoulders square. A storm in repose.

Then, slowly, carefully, reverently, she dipped her head forward.

She bowed like someone answering the ache that had lived too long in silence, with acknowledgment of what it had cost, and defiant gratitude for the voice she'd claimed in return. When she straightened, her breath shook, but her hands didn't.

People who had whispered about her now cheered for her, and at the very edge of the space, just beyond the circle of light, Clinton watched.

Still.

Unmoving.

Mesmerized.

Not because she had won, but because she had risen.

He saw her not as Mystique. Not merely a client. Not even just the woman he loved, but as something larger...A spark wrapped in skin. A stitch stitched from sunlight and fury. A mosaic of every broken dream she'd painstakingly re-pieced into armor.

She had rewritten the narrative they'd once buried her beneath, and from this moment forward? Every silhouette, every hemline, every stage would know her name.

Taylor Rousseau.

Epilogue

Taylor & Clinton

The sewing machines buzzed in sync with the hum of low conversation. Chalk dust softened the edges of color-coded cutting mats. A steamer hissed gently in the corner, and somewhere between the second fitting room and the fabric wall, a playlist of French jazz and early 2000s indie floated through the air like punctuation.

Taylor stood at the center of the swirl.

She wore narrow-leg linen trousers rolled at the ankle and a cropped white button-down open at the collar, sleeves pushed haphazardly above her elbows. With a pencil twisted into a low bun, loose strands of half-held hair fell around her face. A measuring tape curled like a lazy cat around her neck.

To the untrained eye, she looked relaxed.

To anyone paying attention, it was clear she was orchestrating a symphony.

"Drape more here," she said, adjusting a sleeve on the mannequin in front of her. "It needs slouch, not swagger."

"Yes! Sorry, got it," muttered the intern beside her, Jules, a brilliant pattern maker with color-coded notebooks and a tendency to ramble when nervous. She scribbled notes on a clipboard already stained with espresso and thread.

Across the studio, someone called, "Taylor? The Madison fitting just moved to two o'clock!"

"Thank you!" she called back without missing a beat.

The space hummed with motion. Laughter. Spools of thread spun beneath sunbeams from the skylights overhead. Dresses hung on floating racks with tags clipped in place. Coffee cups bloomed like wildflowers across every table. The scent of starch, takeout, and lavender soap mingled above it all.

Her studio, which had once felt like risk and prayer, now buzzed with belonging.

Near the entrance, an article hung framed and matted in soft gold. New York Times. Style Section. Bold print declared: *From Shadow to Spotlight: Taylor Rousseau's Threaded Redemption.*

The photo beneath showed her standing tall in front of the projection screen, arms folded, the crowd behind her a soft blur.

She hadn't gotten used to being stopped on the street, or whispered about at styling panels, or having someone's grandmother email the studio personally to say her debut collection made her cry into a martini.

But this? This—her name on the walls, ink-smudged hands pinning a hem, a team of young designers learning by watching her work—this she had always imagined.

And then, the bell over the door chimed.

She looked over her shoulder, a smile already tugging at her lips before she saw him.

Clinton.

He stepped into the studio in a black coat half unbuttoned, warm wind in his hair, and the faintest trace of sleep-deprived smugness around his eyes.

He held out a latte in a recyclable sleeve with her name misspelled, just slightly. It was their thing now.

"Your favorite," he said, tone dry. "Two shots because you're a menace after three, oat instead of almond because I care about your reputation, and cinnamon because I've learned my lesson after the nutmeg incident."

She took it with a smirk, their fingers brushing.

"You're late," she murmured, sipping. "You missed a sock-related meltdown and three tiny miracles involving dart seams and emotionally adjusted zipper choices."

He looked around. "Place is chaos."

"Glamorous chaos," she corrected.

He stepped closer. "Full of interns and questions and ambition, and you, somehow, in the middle of it. Like gravity."

"You're getting sentimental."

He shrugged. "I just know magic when I see it."

She set the latte down. Leaned in slightly.

"Dinner tonight?" he asked, already smiling like he knew what she'd say.

"Only," she said, straightening his collar just because she could, "if you wear something from my first official collection."

He blinked. "You're putting me in a daffodil suit, aren't you?"

"Hemmed to perfection."

He sighed dramatically. "I'm going to look radiant."

"You're going to look like mine."

At that, his smile softened.

He ran his thumb gently along the edge of her wrist. "Then dinner, and maybe something after."

"Only maybe?"

He leaned in, lips a breath from hers. "We'll negotiate."

Laughter echoed from somewhere near the stairs, someone called out a question about trim, and the moment dissolved into motion again before anyone could notice they'd paused.

Taylor stepped back, brushing her knuckles deliberately across his as she returned to her mannequin.

The lights overhead warmed. The music shifted. Between bolts and buttons, she stood in a life entirely her own. Her future was stitched into every seam. In every note on her intern's clipboard. In every glittering swatch of brilliance unfolding around her.

It was full of color and creativity, and it was all hers.

About Amber W. Lynne

An award-winning author from the misty, coffee-scented landscapes of the Pacific Northwest, Amber blends slow-burn tension, heart-tugging emotion, and just the right amount of sweet and heat into every story she writes. The relationships are relatable and her heroines are fierce, independent, and (sometimes) a little stubborn, but they always find the right man to love them.

Fueled by caffeine and an unshakable belief in love, Amber has been crafting stories since childhood, drawn to the way romance can heal, challenge, and transform. When she's not writing, she's playing with her five kids (I KNOW!), helping fellow writers embrace their literary dreams, or spending time with her hubby making a love story of her own.

<u>Ways to stay in touch:</u>

- Subscribe to her Newsletter

- Via email: info@AmberWLynne.com

- Follow on Instagram - AmberLynne.Author

- Follow on Facebook - Amber W. Lynne, Author

Also by Amber W. Lynne

Working For Love

Lanyards & Lariats
Toolbelts & Ties
Spreadsheets & Sprinkles
Gowns & Gavels
Bourbons & Bling
Holly & Heartbeats

Leave a review at your favorite retailer, and sign-up for Amber's newsletter, to get more love stories, sneak peeks, a chance at Beta or ARC reads, and exclusive giveaways.

To find more books by Amber W. Lynne, visit:
https://amberlynneauthor.com

Bourbons & Bling

Working for Love, Book 5

Visit https://AmberLynneAuthor.com and subscribe to our monthly newsletter to receive launch updates, sneak peeks, exclusive giveaways, and early access to beta and ARC reads!

Sunday mornings were not something Ethan Moore associated with children—particularly when they shared his DNA. Now, across from him at a bistro table in Central Park sat Rosie Ann Moore. His daughter.

The wind had tangled her hair into a wild crown. She sipped cocoa cradled in both hands. "Mr. Ethan, why are you wearing a tie to the park?" She slurped, boots swinging a slow-motion assault on the metal chair legs.

Ethan yanked at his tie, wishing he hadn't gone with the purple paisley. "Serious people take their appearance...well, seriously." He said, aiming for authority.

She eyed him over her cup. "You're gonna wreck your pants. Mom says no one trusts a grown-up who wears a suit to the park."

Bailey. She's raising a smart kid...his kid. He reflected in silence, then raised his cup. "Here's to no more suits at the park."

The girl grinned, revealing a missing front tooth that matched the chaotic energy of the fake tattoos running up her arm, and the bedraggled pink tutu drooping over her jeans. They were a sight with him in his pressed charcoal pants, and her in a whirlwind of dirt, tulle, and chaos. Early joggers gave him sympathetic glances.

He ignored them. He hadn't been a good dad to Rosie, and he was hoping to rectify that. Ethan's strategy, if he could call it that, was to let her set the pace. He would prove to Bailey he deserved more time with his daughter by showing up, even if that meant surrendering his dignity to the whims of a nine-year-old with opinions on mud quality. He'd have to go buy a pair of—he shuddered at the thought—jeans for their future adventures.

After breakfast, the plan was to head to the playground. Rosie raced ahead, weaving through puddles, yelping every time she spotted a squirrel. "That one's called Sir Acorns. He's from England!"

Ethan jogged behind her, coat flapping loosely. He became winded embarrassingly fast. This was nothing like boardroom bargaining.

"Watch me!" Rosie shouted, already scrambling up the jungle gym.

Ethan half-smiled, cringing at the thought of how much he'd lost and realizing, with a jolt, that he had a long way to catch up. He'd never done the boyfriend, husband, or dad thing right, not with Bailey, or anyone else.

She hung upside down, arms swinging. "How many monkeys, Mr. Ethan?"

He ticked each squealing swing on his fingers. "Five monkeys."

Rosie squinted. "You're supposed to say two! You and me!"

He almost laughed. "Then two monkeys, one for each of us."

She beamed, and he gave in to the rare, unguarded feeling in his chest. This was better than closing any deal. The easy joy on her face was an instant reward.

His phone buzzed in his pocket. He let Rosie finish dismounting the monkey bars before glancing down, and squinting at an unfamiliar Seattle area code. There was only one person who'd call him from the Emerald City.

He answered, voice cautious. "Moore."

Nothing at first. Then a shallow breath. "Ethan?"

He knew that voice, even roughened by pain and distance. "Rowan?"

"Sorry. I—" A hitch, more breathless now. "I'm at the hospital. Seattle General. They think it's my gallbladder. They said something about a surgery tonight, and I can barely think straight."

"Where's Tiffany?"

"She's at my friend Kim's—" Her voice broke with a gasp.

He straightened, old nerves rising. Rosie was dragging a

stick in the gravel, blonde head glittering in the rare city sun.

"Is it bad?"

"I don't know." Rowan's voice cracked, raw with fear she was trying to hide. "They said 'complicated case.' I just—I need you, Ethan. Tiff needs you."

"I'll come. I'll get the next flight out." Something inside him jolted.

"Okay." A faint wince in her tone, like she hated needing anything from him. "I'd like Tiffany to stay in her own home. She loves Kim's kids, and it's just next-door, but it's not the same."

The relief in her silence made him bite back everything else he wanted to ask. "Text me Kim's number. I'll talk to her."

"Thank you," she whispered.

When the call ended, Ethan bent to Rosie's level, aware of the thundercloud in his own expression. "Hey, Rosie, change of plans."

She eyed him, always too sharp. "You look scared."

He kneeled further, steadying his breath. "I have to go to Seattle for a few days. We're going to get you back to your Mom, but I'll call every night until we can see each other, again."

Rosie pressed her sticky palm to his. "Is it my sister?"

He nearly coughed. Leave it to Bailey's kid to be direct. "Sort of, it's her mom. Tiffany is okay. I just need to go see her now, instead."

"Okay. You should help her. That's what dads do."

Ethan looked at his daughter and realized just how damned lucky he was that Bailey was giving him another chance to be the dad he always should have been. "I had fun today. I'm sorry it ended early."

"Me, too. Tiffany needs you, though. I don't mind sharing. I just wish—"

"I know..." Ethan filled in the pause. "It sucks that you guys are so far apart."

"Mom says not to say 'sucks,' but she's not here." Rosie paused and looked around, before saying, "It does suck."

"We'll keep working to make that better." Ethan glanced at his phone when a text came through. Kim's number. "I don't know how long I'll be in Seattle, but maybe we can plan a visit with your mom so you two can be together while I'm there."

"I'd like that...dad." Rosie nodded, looking as solemn as a kid in a bedraggled tutu can look. "You should bring her chocolate. I think that helps when you're sad."

He ruffled her hair, love muddy and irrational at the edges. "You're smart, kid."

"I know," she said, grinning.

He brought Rosie back to Bailey's place, explaining as much as he could. Bailey looked at him, arms crossed, a question in every hard line of her face, but she didn't stop him. "Don't screw it up," she said as he turned to leave, her warning more protective than a threat.

He watched Rosie and Bailey wave from their front stoop, sunlight glinting on their joined hands, and realized real life never gave you enough warning before it changed everything.

The cab door had barely closed when Ethan pulled out his phone to book a plane ticket west. His hands shook faintly as he typed in his card number, and the flight confirmation arrived just as the taxi cab dropped him off in front of his apartment to pack his bags.

Thirty-four thousand feet above the ground, Ethan pressed his forehead to the cold airplane window. The overhead track lighting painted everything in a tired blue. Outside the window, dusk knifed across the clouds, creating a line between worlds. He drummed his thumb on the tray table, thinking about the cellophane-wrapped candy in his carry-on bag. It'd been his best guess at an olive branch for a daughter who hardly knew him, and a chance to bring a gift from one sister to another. He'd stood at the terminal kiosk for a full five minutes, paralyzed by indecision, before grabbing the biggest chocolate bar he could find. It hadn't felt right. Not big enough, or simply just not...enough.

Somewhere below, in a quiet stretch of Seattle, his daughter slept in a stranger's house. Tiffany's world had fractured with one hospital call, her mother's voice thinned by pain, her routine shattered by an unfamiliar bed. He pictured her curled tight beneath borrowed blankets, small fingers wrapped around that pink unicorn from last year's Christmas photo—the one whose name escaped him completely.

The admission stung. His LinkedIn profile gleamed with achievements: executive titles, seven-figure deals, industry awards that impressed everyone except two little girls who deserved daily bedtime calls and a father who didn't need a medical emergency to board a plane. Tiffany wasn't just his second daughter. She was his second chance to be the father he'd failed to become the first time around.

The last time he'd seen Tiffany in person, she'd hidden behind her mother's legs, glancing up with wary eyes. Until recently, he'd been drifting in and out of the margins of her life at birthday parties or during awkward video calls.

Unlike Rosie, who waded into meeting new people with fists full of frosting and opinions about everything from ballet to barbecue, Tiffany stayed on the edges—softer-spoken, a little haunted in the corners of her smile. The two girls hadn't even known the other existed until a year ago, when the secrets he shared with Bailey had ended up splashed across the front page of every local newspaper.

Now, Tiffany was only a year younger than Rosie at eight years old, but Ethan realized how much he'd missed with her, too. When Bailey gave him a second chance with Rosie, he'd promised himself he'd make room for both his girls when things got simpler, when work allowed.

Now, life had forced his hand.

He felt the ache of regret. It was a physical thing, as real as the cardboard-sleeved coffee cooling in his hand. Not once in all his years of plotting strategies and mergers had he figured out the formula for building trust from a late start.

He wondered how it would feel to walk into Kim's apartment, see Tiffany's small shoulders tense at the sight of him, and have no right to ask her for anything except for *another* chance.

AVAILABLE AT MAJOR BOOK RETAILERS